T0077929

So Ya Wanna Be
An Actor
... Act Like One

JEROLD FRANKS

authorHOUSE®

AuthorHouse™
1663 Liberty Drive
Bloomington, IN 47403
www.authorhouse.com
Phone: 1 (800) 839-8640

Published by AuthorHouse 02/26/2020

ISBN: 978-1-7283-4878-0 (sc)
ISBN: 978-1-7283-4881-0 (e)

Library of Congress Control Number: 2020903924

Print information available on the last page.

This book is printed on acid-free paper.

For
Renee, Ron and Dad

CONTENTS

ABOUT THE AUTHOR

Jerold Franks, current member and Past President of the Casting Society of America, (CastingSociety.com) is an Independent Casting Director, currently residing in Roanoke, Virginia and casting location film and television projects in the southern and northern regions.

A devoted educator, actor's advocate and lecturer he is responsible for countless television, motion picture as well as musical comedy theatre projects.

Franks is most formerly Executive in Charge of Talent and Casting for Twentieth Century Fox Television and is also the former Director of Talent and Casting for Columbia Pictures Television as well as an ABC Daytime Casting Consultant. Highly respected throughout the country, Franks began his career at Universal City Studios (NBC/Universal). Prior to entering casting, he served a two-year stint as a theatrical agent learning the ropes from the other side of the casting desk.

His first casting assignment was a year on the Emmy Award winning half hour sitcom "Barney Miller". Moving on to Warner Brothers Television, he cast Movies of The Week and Mini-series and for the last 25 years has been an independent Casting Director while concurrently teaching acting courses at the University and high school level.

He is currently a full time substitute at William Byrd High and Middle Schools in Vinton, Virginia.

In addition to "Barney Miller" his Emmy recognition includes the short lived CBS series "Kaz" and for the well received 2 Hr. NBC— Wonderful World of Disney production: "A Mother's Courage: The Mary Thomas Story."

Mr. Franks was elected to his third term as international President of the Casting Society of America in January, 1995 after serving three consecutive terms as Vice President. He is a past member of the Executive

Committee for the Media Access office in Los Angeles, an organization that promotes a more realistic view and support of the physically challenged persons in the entertainment industry.

Jerold Franks was honored with the 1997 Award of Excellence for Contributions to the Entertainment Industry by the Southern California Motion Picture Council, the 1989 Award of Excellence by the California Governor's Committee for employment of the physically challenged persons for his casting of the television movie of the week "Kids Like These".

A three time Emmy acknowledged Casting Director, he is the 1989 recipient of the ARTIOS Award, the Casting Society of America's highest honor, for his casting of the feature film "Bagdad Café." His 2004 ABC Touchstone pilot "LOST" which he cast in Hawaii in collaboration with his Los Angeles colleague April Webster garnered a Golden Globe and Casting Emmy for best new series.

In addition, Jerry Franks serves on the advisory Board of the Deaf Entertainment Foundation, is a consultant for New York Equity fundraisers and continues his active year round work on behalf of The Actors Fund of America, the Pat Tillman Foundation (pattillman.org) as well as St. Judas Children's Hospital and RXLaughter(.org) on which she serves as a Board Member.

He has been honored by (to include) The City of Hope, Cedars Sinai Hospital, The Thalians Mental Health Hospital, Childhelp USA, countless AIDS Foundations, the American Heart Association, Diabetes Research Foundation at the City of Hope, the NAACP and the White House for his tireless humanitarian efforts and accomplishments.

He was honored with the "Vision" Award for Lifetime Achievement in Casting by the Virginia Film Festival in April of 2005.

Mr. Franks received the Lifetime Humanitarian Award from Cedar's Sinai Hospital in Los Angeles on October 7, 2006 as well as the NAACP's "Men of Honor" Award in 2007.

Mr. Franks holds graduate degrees in Theatre Arts and Clinical Psychology and has served on the faculties of the University of California, Los Angeles, UCLA, Cypress College, California State University, Los Angeles, Long Beach and Northridge, American University, and Wesleyan University.

Additionally he guests lectures country wide with his book "So Ya Wanna Be An Actor…Act Like One."

Franks is currently on a book tour benefiting St. Judes Children's Hospital and RXLaugher Children's cancer Clinic at UCLA (Los Angeles). (June 2014)

As an author, Jerry Franks presents with forthright accuracy, honesty, integrity and humor an expert presentation of getting the break and how to continue growing as a person and as an actor.

"So Ya Wanna Be an Actor…Act Like One" will diminish many anxieties which the up and coming actor feel, as the book presents the most honest inside information ever written. Franks has been deemed an "actor's advocate" and his invaluable experiences are shared with modesty and candidness.

**Ranked among Backstage West top 10 best books for 2002 . . . .
Rev: 12/04
Rev: 5/05
Rev: 6/06
Rev: 12/2013

In the May 2, 2013, the trade paper Variety (trade paper reports on tv and film) author Cynthia Littleton reports: "The state of the agency biz."

Ask any agent at any shop, boutique or behemoth of the state of the 'ten percenter biz and he or she will earnestly say, "It's all about the clients." Of course, that's been true for Hollywood talent reps

Since the days of Abe Lastfogel (original founder WM Agency) But in the last five years the role of the agent and business of running a sizable agency has been buffeted by monumental changes spurred by seismic shift in the broader entertainment landscape.

Top agents are on the front lines trying to figure out how to make money off of cell-phone screens and the like. It's an alien landscape that is calling for them to see around corners in ways that are even vexing the industry's sharpest CEO's. The emergence of WMA (William Morris Agency) as a superpower to challenge the hegemony of CAA (Creative Artists Agency) has altered the talent representation playing field for everyone....agents."

For the last 75 years, since the Academy Players Directory came into existence, people worldwide have been asking: "how do I become an actor?" The Academy Players Director consists of four books containing thousands of photos with contact information for actors in all categories: leading men/leading women/children/character actors.

"Why am I an advocate of stage and daytime drama?" Learning a new script each night for the next day's production or studying drama and comedy in the theatre can only help to prepare an actor for success.

What is non-traditional casting? What do you mean tv shows and film want "real?

I am in hopes that this book will serve you all well in any and all areas of the tv and motion picture industry.

It never occurred to me that the book would be successful-so here we are 13 years laterand one asks, "has the business changed a lot?"-Well, duh-yes. It has changed "monumentally".

FOR PARENTS ONLY

While scanning Explore Talent (Virginia) I saw an ad for IMTC – "International Model and Talent For Christ." Billboard and print ads. I couldn't believe my eyes. To have a company use Christ's name as a sales pitch personally offended me and I sent a note off to the Screen Actors Guild.

"...the very moment they ask for any money up front, say 'thank you' and leave the office." jf

Several weekends ago I was casting a faith based film at Liberty University in Lynchburg, Virginia.

While researching the talent pool in Lynchburg and and surrounding areas, I came upon an the above mentioned ad that mentioned "Christ" in the advertisement for an upcoming local workshop.

How dare anyone use Jesus Christ's name to have young people and struggling parents spend thousands of dollars for a day of meeting with people who will prance them across a stage with a panel consisting of perhaps a casting director, agent, personal manager or photographer.

RIP OFF. Parents "please, please be leary if there are costs involved with promises when signing up for acting workshops.

In February of 2014, I was casting a film on location in my current city of Roanoke, Virginia. I advertised on both Breakdown Express as well as the Virginia members of EXPLORE talent. I highly recommend both for your photo and contact information.

EXPLORE TALENT (see website) is a great tool for casting director's on location. Country wide, there is no better). For the larger cities, there is no better resource that matches BREAKDOWN SERVICES,

LTD. This company is the bible for casting director's as well as actors, producers, directors – the whole gamut of a script.

Breakdown Services as well as their offshoots of 'actor's express', is the casting director's best tool for casting – even in the regions. Many budgets hold money to fly actors all over the country and all over the world. Explore Talent gives a c.d. an idea of what the bank of talent is in each respective city.

Every state in the Union is abundant with actor scams— dishonest promises and dream breaking guarantees. Scam artists preying on the emotions and dreams of hundreds of thousands of young people earn millions of dollars a year. I, along with others in our acting community, the Unions and private organizations, are attempting to protect you—the aspiring actor.

Please read carefully about the effort and work it takes in the acting profession. With the advent of the super highway in our computer world— anyone can get a diploma in any subject they wish—pretty good scam— but—I wonder how these people sleep at night? Pretty dishonest—don't you think? The bottom line is "they're only kidding themselves

If you are reading this book to find the magic bullet for making it in the profession of acting, read no further. There is no magic, no panacea, and no mystery to the business. The profession of acting is just that—a profession.

You CAN become successful, you CAN achieve the dreams you've had since the first time you stood in front of a mirror rehearsing an Oscar speech, you CAN achieve the joyous rewards which go into the most exciting, challenging, frustrating, anxiety producing, wonderful profession in the world—IF—all of the elements fit together. Talent, tenacity, patience and the ability to learn and to get your ego out of the way, some luck or Karma and a great deal of work. Study hard, hope you have talent, strive to make yourself a better person through life experience and education, because that is part of what it takes to become a working actor. In reading this book, hopefully I can help each and every one of you to prepare and learn how to become a working actor. There is no guarantee. I, like many people in your lifetime will only be a tiny component to the overall finished product. YOU are the one that must come through and produce the goods. It is YOU, the individual, who must grab all of these components and elements and put them all together. I offer no promises. No one can ever offer promises of success . . . that is your responsibility. Talent is either natural or it must be nurtured and even the most gifted, knowledgeable and experienced actors still study, learn, and continue to grow.

This book was not designed as a "positive thinking and you'll get there" book. It was put together with great thought garnered from many years of experience. I will hopefully try to save you anguish which you with my often bluntness. I pull no punches.

I suggest that in order to accomplish what you want so desperately, you have to learn the secret. you want to be an actor like one! And acting like an actor has a lot to do with the reality of whether you have what it takes to get there and whether or not you are willing to go after it. And 'acting like an actor'— means study and hard work—just like any other 'profession'.

*A note from Jerry There are many names throughout this book whom some of you may not recognize—go to http:// www.Imdb.com and you will get a sense of who is and was out there for both you and for me. I've been very lucky in my career to have worked with and met some of the greats of our profession. I wish all of you the very same success.

If you have any unanswered questions, which I may have overlooked, please feel free to contact me at JeroldFranksCSA@aol.com. I sincerely hope that this book will make you think and grow and perhaps help some of you aspire to your dreams.

The last piece of advice I can offer you is "to be realistic". You will know in your gut if you are cut out for the very difficult and competitive field of show biz.

May, 2000
May, 2005—rev.
June, 2006—rev.

CHAPTER ONE

My Parents Think I'm Crazy

I decided in this edition to include my own personal experiences with people I had met during my career and how I noticed no matter what level of income or socio-economic level one comes from-if it is meant for you to be a successful actor...then it will be. Remember that. Luck as well as my own personal philosophy of "You are where you are supposed to be and in the position you are currently. "We" have nothing to do about it.

I would ask that you pay attention to the chapter on FAME and being anointed. You will understand.

I lucked out. My parents supported whatever I wanted to do in life.

The only advice my Dad gave me has afforded me a happy life. My Dad said "I don't care if you "dig ditches for a living, just love what you do and be happy to get up in the a.m." And, at this stage of my life-I am very happy.

I feel like full circle-In high school, I directed our senior play and now I am back in the classroom as well as being involved in school productions and doing some location casting.

The other piece of advice was "get a degree in something you can fall back on."

Thus-I will support any actor I meet-however, they must have a back-up plan. Mine was teaching as well as becoming a licensed psychologist.

All The President's children – nepotism does not matter

My assistant buzzed me as I was in the middle of concentrating on a lead role: 'Jerry, John Kennedy Jr. is on the phone. "It's not Kennedy-it's

Clooney-please tell him that I'll phone him back." This reference is to George Clooney-the king of pranks.

'Jerry, it doesn't sound like Clooney-I think you might want to take this.'

Ok. thanks. "Hello, this is Jerry Franks. May I help you?" 'Hello, Mr. Franks, this is John Kennedy, Jr.

My Aunts Ethel and Eunice suggested that I phone you. I hope I'm not intruding on your time.'

The year was 1979-John was in college taking a theatre class and quite frankly word had gotten out that he wanted to be an actor. I seem to remember that every agent in town was after him.

'How might I help you John?' Well, I am pursuing a career in acting and my mother and I don't seem to see eye to eye.

'John-let me cut to the bottom line. I will give you any support and advice you need and I am flattered that you would call me-BUT-you need to have a backup career-and I must take your Mom's side.'

John became an attorney-went into the magazine business and never pursued acting-but I sense that 'perhaps' he would have gone into politics-which might serve his acting chops well. Had he become an actor, I sense that he would have been up there with the most revered leading men throughout history.

CHAPTER ONE – 'MY PARENTS THINK I'M CRAZY"

"Are you crazy??' my own parents asked? Not only your parents think you might be crazy when you decide to announce that you want to become an actor. We can include friends, neighbors, significant others and anyone else who passes through your life on a regular basis. I have tried guiding my younger friends, colleagues and associates not to sit in judgment. Do as you wish with no one else's input and if you ask for other's input, at the very bottom line is your own instinct. My producer friend Dennis Johnson's Granny used to say "Instinct is God whispering in your ear". You should trust your instinct and DO discuss your decision with your parents so they understand your goals. You "might" get resistance, threats, drama, major upset and crisis. Then on the other hand, you just might be surprised that your parents do support your dreams just like the parents of Josh Lucas, George Clooney and Leonardo DiCaprio, Ben Affleck, and so many of the up and coming newcomers. Maybe you will be a newcomer at some time in your life.

When I was eighteen years old I dropped out of college for a year and moved to Los Angeles. Within a month I was filing purchase orders at Universal City Studios. It was not what I imagined Hollywood held for me. My fantasy was a paneled office complete with a fireplace and me as some Vice President holding court to all of the famous stars. I had no conception that I was entering a "profession" like any other—and I would have to work diligently to succeed. Following my initial interview with the personnel department, I weaseled my way onto the actual studio lot to get a glimpse of what show business was really about.

Adorning the main street of the Universal back lot were the dressing rooms of Tony Randall, Alfred Hitchcock, Doris Day,

Rock Hudson along with famous Hollywood producers— including Marlon Brando, Sr. I rushed home to call my parents to tell them how much I wanted to be in "show biz." "Are you crazy!" What about college, they responded? How can you do this? "Does this sound familiar? The bottom line is that though my parents were terribly unhappy about me entering the business (a business they knew nothing about), they were actually supportive in their own way. My parents are now both deceased, but my Dad did live long enough to see my happiness in my career. would not lower her pride, even to her own parents, whom she loved so dearly. She wanted to do her thing and her thing was show business. Many of you have (or will have) many similar stories. Address the issue of what your parents and others will think or say and remember. The choice lies with you and no one else. Not convinced, pick up a book called "What you think of me is none of my business". "What do I do with the guilt?" You ask. Forget it! If you feel so deeply that the bug has bitten you, go for it! You must ask yourself, "Am I doing what I really want to do?" or are you doing something because someone else wants me to? (See chapter—Beware the wrath of Jerry Franks).When I left my proposed studies in Psychology to go into "show biz" my parents were not happy. Yet, once they got used to the idea, they were totally supportive. Remember, your parents have had their shot in life and you are going to be around a lot longer than they, so do what you want to do. It took me many years of therapy along with life experience to discover that unhappiness stems from doing something that you hate doing. While the anguish and anxiety prevailed in the early days of my career, it was worth it at the end. This is heavy-duty stuff dealing with flesh, blood and emotions. I have learned through years in the business that one must strive for that which one desires (that was deep). As actors, or potential actors, the one rule you must remember at all times is that acting is a profession. It is a business just like any other business. One must gain knowledge of show business first, then act on that knowledge. If you want to be an actor, I suggest you get a back-up plan—get a degree—in something—even acting (theatre). Follow the legendary George Burns advice. He says, "If you want to live a long happy life, fall in love with what you do for a living." While lecturing, I always not only recommend, but insist that those going into the profession of acting, get a college degree in something they enjoy—some day, you might want to leave acting and pursue other avenues—be prepared. Some of you will have support from those closest to you. Unfortunately, some of you will not. This book is not intended to tantalize you into acting. It is written to help you visualize the realities of acting and what hardships you might face. And quite frankly, forget any hardships—it's tough, tough work. I always compare the profession of acting to the professions of medicine, law, politics, Harvard University, Yale and striving for a Noble Prize. Many of you believe that your parents were short sighted and manipulative or just didn't care.

You just have to acknowledge that fact and get over it. As a college professor once told me, "When it comes to parenting, if you do it this way (hand extended pointing to the right) or if you do it this way (hand extended pointing to the left), you can never get it right!" If you wish to use that pain as a motivator for your "acting emotions" then fine, but do not bring that "poor me", negative, doomsayer, cocky attitude into a casting directors office. First of all, casting directors don't really care. So just be yourself and don't be such a downer and you will be all right nd "leave your ego outside of the office". Acting takes talent, which needs to be nurtured. Then, that nurtured talent needs to be used on it's own. You cannot become a surgeon without going through training. I must repeat that acting is a profession and must be treated as one. That means that there is a great deal of hard work ahead, many hours of fear, insecurity, questioning and all of the things that we worry about when embarking on a new challenge. It's like going to a your job on the first day when you know no one and feel like the lowest rung on the latter. Not to mention reading, studying, research and continuous discipline, both mentally and physically. If a person wanting to enter the profession of acting is passionate, devoted, dedicated, willing to study, willing to sacrifice, and has talent, the chances are higher in achieving the goal of becoming an actor. Talent must be nurtured. Be realistic and honest enough with yourself to recognize your own talent. You may not have it. If you do not have it, you must be honest enough to acknowledge that fact.

Get your ego out of the way! Don't fall into the category of being a "would-be" actor all of your life. I was speaking to a group of actors recently who were 40 to 70 years of age with one or two credits on their resume. One of the questions that came up was, "When do you give up trying to make it?" My response was f you wake up in your 40's with a credit or two on your resume and no agent or personal manager—it's time to rethink your career I was more than impressed with Jodie Foster and Brooke Shields who went to college in the middle of very hot careers. What they majored in is not the point. The point is that they have degrees to fall back on. For me, I did return to school and obtained my Master's Degree in Psychology—MY own personal backup plan. I've been quoted so many times saying that I have more respect for New York actors than any other in the country. Why? In New York, an actor is always taking class—whether it be scene study, dance, voice, or movement.

They are non-stop—pounding the pavement. So you have no money? Then get into a play. Free training and the most solid training. Don't be lazy and stop making excuses. You can work a gig at Starbuck's, appear in a play—and hopefully be seen by someone who can boost your career. the bottom line to this chapter is: a) have a backup plan(career) and b) try it at any age so you don't wake up one day and ask yourself "I wonder what would have happened if I had 'taken a risk?' c) be totally realistic about your acting career-it is either paying off or you need to address your backup plan. jf 2013

CHAPTER TWO

What Do You Really Want? To Say You're An Actor Or To Be One??

— — — — — —

For those of you who know me as of 2013, you probably only know me as substitute teacher in Vinton, Virginia.

I'll take a minute to give you a brief background of my experiences before lucking into casting, thanks to my friend and colleague Lori Openden who kept her promise. Keeping your word, your integrity and your respect are adjectives of which I was reminded when I served as an agent in the earliest days of my casting career.

Prior to entering "show biz", I was a psychologist for many years, both in private practice and on the staff at the Veterans Administration Hospital in w. Los Angeles, California.

I dreamed of being a surgeon, or so I thought. Due to economic realities, and my "challenges" in chemistry, I quickly changed majors and became engulfed in the world of human behavior. In looking back, I sense that this was my first "lucky" break in my career.

After much soul searching I finally came in touch with why I was so unhappy counseling people. I was more impressed with what the title of Jerold Franks—the psychologist looked like rather than what the job entailed.

The point: Do you simply like saying that you're an actor or do you really want to be one? If you do really want to be one then get ready to work your asses off. And again, I caution—this is no guarantee—remember—it takes many components to get there and even more to stay in the mainstream.

If you don't want to commit totally to your profession by getting into theatre productions or taking classes in cold readings, scene study or voice then don't even bother. If you are young and starting out, then priority number one is being able to support yourselves while "going to school." Acting is a profession—I will repeat this statement many times throughout this book. In any profession, comes study—schooling— coursework, internships and patience.

I don't believe in the term
  "paying your dues"—I believe in the expression "paying for experience". In my opinion, I believe that in this day and age and marketplace of films and television along with demographics and societal values and peer pressure, looks and age do count more than being an accomplished actor. Let me qualify by saying that the "look"-the "it" factor counts more when starting out. The "look" is part of the "it"—If you wish to be considered part of that distinguished group that have the "look" and the "acting skills", get ready to do your homework. In close to 30 years of casting I have never seen the competition as demanding as it is now in the 21st century. As you make a passionate promise to yourself to succeed in this profession called acting, make certain that you watch yourself at every turn.

  The very first rule in this profession is that you do not ever pay up front for any services. This includes representation, consultations, and guarantee of agents and guarantee of work. Pay nothing up front except maybe a deposit for a photo session, and you don't pay your agent for a photo session. You pay the photographer directly. Many a scam offers consults, photos, and recommendations—forget it. Please pay for NOTHING up front.

  When I finally completed my studies in psychology at UCLA and Boston University, I was going to be cruising on easy street. I thought there would be no more studying, no more lectures, no more authority figures to deal with, no more competition, and no more ego-crazed people—Boy was I wrong! Not only wrong, but also dumb, ignorant and an e. I worked harder than ever before and still had problems keeping up with all of it. Lots of hopeful actors arrive in Hollywood and get jobs as waiters. They figure that they will just work as a waiter and hopefully land an acting job by virtue of their looks. It is a very admirable for a young talent to work hard at a job while trying to become a successful actor. Yet, one must study acting in some aspect while working.

To say that you are an actor while you are not studying, working at acting in any form, meeting people in the field, but simply only waiting around for someone to discover you is bullshit. Get your ass into class and tell people that you are studying to be an actor. After you have completed your first play or uttered your first line in a production you must continue to study and one day—you might be able to say, "I am an actor". When, you ask?

After you are supporting yourself with acting work. If actors like Pacino or Streep can go to class and keep their craft sharp, so can you. My actor friend, Joe Lando, came into my office for a reading. He was upset that he wasn't getting many parts. This guy has the looks, had the passion and was taking class—to no avail. I told him to go back to New York and get into classes and theatre.

Next time I heard from him, he has landed a soap opera role and proceeded to make the crossover to nighttime and worked many a job thereafter. Joe knew that he had to sharpen his craft, so he became responsible. By the way, Joe Lando was the second lead to Jane Seymour in the long running CBS Emmy Award winning show—"Dr. Quinn, Medicine Woman"

There was a guy who grew up in the San Fernando Valley of Los Angeles County. He tried acting in Hollywood and it just wasn't working for him, so according to the inside scoop, he conferred with a casting director buddy and made the decision to do something about his problem. He moved off to New York and worked his ass off in theatre and got his big break. This guys name is Kevin Spacey and the rest is history. What does it mean to say that I am an actor as opposed to really being one? What does one do to really become an actor? How do I know whether or not I really want to become an actor? Am I passionate about my craft? Does the glamour and affectation associated with Hollywood get in my way of becoming a real actor?

When will I let people know that I am not an actor anymore, but a tree farmer?

When you study, remember to be you. Do not copy another actor.

However I do suggest that you watch the actors techniques, comedic timing, movement, eyes, and watch how they carry themselves.

When I speak to large groups of actors I usually ask, "How many of you think that you will become stars?" and 99% of them raise their hands. Get a grip! If one out of the large group becomes a "star" I would be pleased. However, it is very possible for the 99% to become good working actors and make a good living.

CHAPTER THREE

For Parents Only

"...the very moment they ask for any money up front, say 'thank you' and leave the office." Jerry Franks

Several weekends ago I was casting a faith based film at Liberty University. While researching talent pools in Lynchburg and and surrounding areas, I came upon a ad that mentioned "Christ" in the full name of the workshop How dare anyone use Jesus Christ's name to have young people and struggling parents spend thousands of dollars for a day of meeting with people who will prance them across a stage with a panel consisting of perhaps a casting director, agent, personal manager or photographer.

RIP OFF.

In February of 2014, I was casting a film on location in my current city of Roanoke, Virginia. I advertised on both Breakdown Express as well as the Virginia members of EXPLORE talent. I highly recommend both for your photo and contact information.

EXPLORE TALENT (see website) is a great tool for casting director's on location. Country wide, there is no better). For the larger cities, there is no better any resource that matches BREAKDOWN SERVICES,

LTD. This company is the bible for casting director's as well as actors, producers, directors – the whole gamut of a script.

Breakdown Services as well as their offshoots of 'actor's express' the casting director's best tool for casting – even in the regions. Many budgets hold money to fly actors all over the country and all over the world. Explore Talent gives a c.d. an idea of what the bank of talent is in each respective city.

While scanning Explore Talent (Virginia) I saw an ad for IMTC – "International Model and Talent For Christ." Billboard and print ads. I couldn't believe my eyes. To have a company use Christ's name as a sales pitch would make <u>me</u> run in the opposite direction.

Every state in the Union is abundant with actor scams— dishonest promises and dream breaking guarantees. Scam artists preying on the emotions and dreams of hundreds of thousands of young people earn millions of dollars a year. I, along with others in our acting community, the Unions and private organizations, are attempting to protect you—the aspiring actor.

Please read carefully about the effort and work it takes in the acting profession. With the advent of the super highway in our computer world— anyone can get a diploma in any subject they wish—pretty good scam— but—I wonder how these people sleep at night? Pretty dishonest—don't you think? The bottom line is "they're only kidding themselves

If you are reading this book to find the magic bullet for making it in the profession of acting, read no further. There is no magic, no panacea, and no mystery to the business. The profession of acting is just that—a profession.

You CAN become successful, you CAN achieve the dreams you've had since the first time you stood in front of a mirror rehearsing an Oscar speech, you CAN achieve the joyous rewards which go into the most exciting, challenging, frustrating, anxiety producing, wonderful profession in the world—IF—all of the elements fit together. Talent, tenacity, patience and the ability to learn and to get your ego out of the way, some luck or Karma and a great deal of work. Study hard, hope you have talent, strive to make yourself a better person through life experience and education, because that is part of what it takes to become a working actor. In reading this book, hopefully I can help each and every one of you to prepare and learn how to become a working actor. There is no guarantee. I, like many people in your lifetime will only be a tiny component to the overall finished product. YOU are the one that must come through and produce the goods. It is YOU, the individual, who must grab all of these components and elements and put them all together. I offer no promises. No one can ever offer promises of success . . . that is your responsibility. Talent is either natural or it must be nurtured and even the most gifted, knowledgeable and experienced actors still study, learn, and continue to grow.

This book was not designed as a "positive thinking and you'll get there" book. It was put together with great thought garnered from many years of experience. I will hopefully try to save you anguish which you with my often bluntness. I pull no punches.

I suggest that in order to accomplish what you want so desperately, you have to learn the secret. you wanna be an actor like one! And acting like an actor has a lot to do with the reality of whether you have what it takes to get there and whether or not you are willing to go after it. And 'acting like an actor'— means study and hard work—just like any other 'profession'.

*A note from Jerry There are many names throughout this book whom some of you may not recognize—go to http:// www.Imdb.com and you will get a sense of who is and was out there for both you and for me. I've been very lucky in my career to have worked with and met some of the greats of our profession. I wish all of you the very same success.

If you have any unanswered questions, which I may have overlooked, please feel free to contact me at JeroldFranksCSA@aol.com. I sincerely hope that this book will make you think and grow and perhaps help some of you aspire to your dreams.

May, 2000
May, 2005—rev.
June, 2006—rev.

CHAPTER FOUR

Parents Of Young Children— Bewear
The Rath Of Jerry Franks

— — — — — —

Now that we have discussed you as an adult and issues you may or may not have with your parents—rejection, disappoint, perhaps support—I want to address the parents who want their young children to get into show biz. In 1984, my late twin sister Susan Crow, who later became a successful children's agent, sat in our offices, opening envelopes and trying to learn the business. Susan had a good eye—BUT—when she approached me with the idea that my only nephew Scott—

"should" be an actor, I looked at her like she was the psychotic of our family. "Are you crazy? Why the hell would you put this kid (then 12 years old) in this world of such stress and disappointment? Well, not to belabor the story—she arranged to have Scott appear in a couple of TV shows—an extra, a one liner—he hated it—we all discussed it—and that was the end of that dream. But whose dream was it—certainly not my nephew's who went on to become a top-notch computer wiz— but it was the dream of my sister. Al Onorato and I have won several awards in casting children so I frequently visited our reception area to greet and to observe parents and their behavior with their children. I must note here that my Masters Degree is in Child Psychology and I went on through the years, coursework after coursework to become what is known as a "child specialist". What is a child specialist—I think it's one who is an expert at changing diapers and having some kind of psychic connection to children of all ages. I can get any kid to look at me and smile—and it is one of the great joys of my life. Moving along—if you could be a fly on the wall and experience some of the incidences in my reception office, you'd either slap the parent across the face or call the Child Welfare office. To you the parent who so desperately want to give your child the opportunity to achieve success and money—please, look at your motivation. There was a recent "promo" for one of the reality shows—I believe it was Fear Factor a mother telling a child to shut up and stop being frightened of whatever this "stunt" was—upcoming. I almost through a rock at the TV. What was this mother thinking? I ask that you as parents really look at your hidden agendas. Are you trying to fulfill your own dream that didn't happen? Are you fulfilling your child's dream? Are you looking at the bucks? I highly suggest and recommend that you be honest in your thinking. My two favorite children in my personal life are my pals—Zachary and Brianna (Breezie). I love them with all of my heart and would go to any length in life to make them happy. Like any parent,

Grandparent, Aunt, and Uncle, significant other to the child— we want the best for the children in our lives. Walter Cronkite reminded me in an interview with Barbara Walters about how we feel about our respective children. Barbara was interviewing Mr. Cronkite and at the end of the interview she chided him on the fact that he had become a Grandfather for the very first time—late in life. Here is the gist (not ver batIm) of the interview: "Walter, I understand that there is a happy event in your life, the birth of your first Grandchild!" Mr. Cronkite:—

"Why yes, Barbara, it is a very special time for us". Barbara—

"How wonderful—and what is your Grandchild's name? Mr.

Cronkite—" Well, Barbara, he has the same name as every other Grandchild . . . . "Perfect". Yes, all of us think of our babies or young children as perfect, because quite frankly—they are—to us. However that does not give us free license to push them into a profession in which they have no interest and quite frankly, a profession which might leave them permanently scarred in later years. Anna Duke (Patty Duke) is an example of a tormented childhood—despite the fact that she is gifted—always was and it took her years of therapy and support to become a happy adult.

Getting back to Zach and Breezie. These two children are the product of their father, Joel, an aspiring actor who became like a kid brother to me—and then Lisa—Mommie—whom I adore like a daughter and who herself was exposed to the in's and outs of showbiz working at NBC in

Burbank for many years. When Zachary, now referred to as "Z" was about two years old, Lisa got the idea to put him into commercials. Well, I being the first to admit that this child is perfect, was dead set against it, but—

Lisa prevailed and started taking "Z" out on "modeling/print assignments. He was perfectly proportioned and fit into any outfit off the rack and with his incredible blue eyes, white blonde hair and chubby cheeks—he was like a Gerber baby. After three or four "interviews"—"Z" made it perfectly clear to Lisa that this was not for him. To this day, I'm very proud of Lisa for her wisdom in not pushing the kid into something that made him unhappy.

Now we get to Breezie, who informed me when she was 4 years old long ago that she wanted to be "a movie star". Well, Ucknee (the name deemed me when "Z" began talking, "I want to be a movie star" and proceeded to change outfits 19 or 20 times to show me what roles she could play. The more that I listened to her (then 4y/o) the more I believed that perhaps she really wanted to try for a career in acting.

She was working hard—ballet and tap lessons, a performance in "The Nutcracker"—reading, listening, and pretending. Note that her parents support her dreams and Breezie is learning not to be disappointed. She is learning and growing and in this case, I support her efforts. Now—stage mothers—get off of your child's back—don't promise rewards if they "audition"—don't tell them that they will become stars: be a responsible parent. Do they like acting? Do they have any talent? Are you supporting and pushing your child because you did not achieve or accomplish your own dreams? Be honest— this is your child's emotional well being at stake. Paul Petersen*

(The Donna Reed Show) has an organization called "A Minor Consideration"—which can be located at www.PaulPetersen.com.

Paul's organization explains how to protect the rights of children and is perhaps one of the most important sources for children's rights in the industry today.

I cannot in good conscience ever refer vaguely to children's talent and modeling competitive "events."

* see www.Imdb.com for Paul Petersen's credits and credentials.

P.S. Now in 2014, in checking FACEBOOK, 'Breezie' has posted two or three songs – apparently she Inherited her vocal abilities from her Dad.

CHAPTER FIVE

I Just Got Off The Bus—Now What Do I Do?

- - - - - -

Every day of the year aspiring actors everywhere get off trains, planes, buses and out of automobiles and relocate to L.A. or N.Y.

I have met countless of these brave, starry-eyed kids. If you could visualize yourself in any city new to you without having: any professional contacts any family connections any close friends no car little money and no job—then let me suggest that either you like to live on the edge or you are what we in showbiz refer to as a "loose cannon." Take your pick. Why do you want to leave the security of a small town, or even a big city, both of which offer the reality of making a living, and try to make it in the "biz?" If you were anything like me then you will know what I am saying when I suggest that it was intrinsically in my blood and that there was nothing I could do about it. Call it creativity if you will. Please make a note that I never wanted to be an actor. It wasn't because I did not have respect for the acting profession; after all, I deal with actors on a regular basis. I simply had more fun behind the scenes.

ALL THAT SKIN – ALL THAT LANGUAGE-

My good friend Ted Cordes, NBC's former Sr. Vice President – Standards and Practices and I share the exact same viewpoint on the 'decline of good taste' in the movie or TV business. Sad – here's what Mr.

Cordes says:

"TV attitudes on sex and sexual language really changed with the Clinton/Lewinsky scandal.

When news started such as reporting of oral sex, audience expectation made a drastic change.

The is a prime element in speeches I make in schools and interviews."

Actors get their jollies in front of the camera or the audience while I preferred working in the trenches trying to "assist"—I have always thought I was born to teach. Let's be realistic and again let me remind you that acting is a business. It has become more of a business in the last few years in particular because major corporations are buying up studios, production companies and networks.

Make the decision on whether or not you want your life to be bought and sold by large corporations in order to make it big. It hurts me, as a sensitive human being, to see young and inexperienced kids stepping off the latter of dreams and ending up with the proverbial shark following them as soon as they jump off into the water (with no life raft available).

Throughout the country you can pick up a magazine or a newspaper and read an ad that says, "Be An Actor Overnight Success Is Just A Plane Trip Away, etc." One will see these ads anywhere you go. Now, some ads are legit, but most are not. Do not waste your time, money, and energy. You need to know with whom you're dealing. (See chapter Scams' R Us) The acting business has many sides. In the "normal" world, when you open up a business you must choose partners that you trust to make the business operate successfully. If you plan to enter the acting profession you must encourage it—But before you do, let's take a look at the many variables involved. Let's examine whether you belong in acting. Let's see if you know the in and outs of the struggles and frustrations that are involved. Do you realize the hard work that is involved? It reminds me of my eighth grade teacher in Bradley Beach, NJ, Miss Kofel, and the course she gave on professions. I was hell bent on becoming a surgeon, there was no turning back, and my mind was made up. The problem was that I didn't realize how important the understanding of chemistry was to the medical profession. The point of my story is that I wanted to be a surgeon but I chose not to kill myself with the struggles of learning chemistry. I spent 5 days registering for pre-med courses and one day dropping out.

I have seen the most talented dramatic actors want desperately to do comedy. I am talking about good actors. The comedy just wasn't there. No "intrinsic humor". Don't push it. Work in an area that is most comfortable to you. (read 'Soar With Your Strengths') For those of you trying to decide whether or not you really want to make it in the acting profession, read on and become knowledgeable of all of the trials and tribulations you will face. Be realistic about all that you know nothing about.

This is one of the toughest professions to enter, succeed and sustain. Be absolutely sure that you want it badly enough, make sure the passion is there and that the sacrifice is worth it.

CHAPTER SIX

It's Not What You Know It's Who You Know

1975 might have been one of the worst years of my life professionally. I was a theatrical agent. Not my cup of tea I learned after a couple of years. For 30 years, actors have asked the same question with respect to agents and personal managers.

Do you only work with certain agents? Do you only hire actors if they are with the larger agencies and with the more powerful agents? Well, the answer for me is NO. I work and have always worked with virtually ever agent and personal manager in Los Angeles and New York. The exception to the rule in working with an agent is if they "stick" me—once is okay—twice—bye bye. HOWEVER, if there is an actor whom I wish to meet and they happen to be with one of these agents with whom I don't trust, I do get the actor into my office, whether it be through the agent or by contacting the actor directly. The rule in the agency business is that you are as important to the agency in relation to the amount of money you bring in annually. The new trend in the agency world is—if an actor hasn't booked within 6 months—they are dropped from the agency. I was really looking for a transition in my profession. I thought that I might want to become a casting director. In the 70's there were not that many half-hour projects so the casting directors were not as competitive with each other. There was plenty of work for everyone. Lori Openden, former Senior Vice President of Talent and Casting for NBC, was casting Barney Miller at the time. I shared with Lori my interest in trying to find a casting position and Lori told me that she would keep her eye out. As it turned out, Lori was offered a position with MTM Television and as promised, she called me to see if I was interested in interviewing for the Barney Miller casting director position. Of course I was excited and thrilled and happily accepted the opportunity to meet with the Executive Producer/Creator, Danny Arnold. I got the job and from *Barney Miller* my casting career began. I've always been very grateful to Lori who was and still remains a good friend and colleague. My Uncle Lew always told me, "It's not what you know, it's who you know." Well, first off all, grammatically it is whom you know, but let me clue you in.

Once you get in the door, you could be a relative of the Pope, but if you can't cut it, you will be cut.

Hollywood actors are notorious for grandstanding and recommending to friends, "Oh, just call my very close friend Joe Schmoe and he will hook you up. Forget it! It doesn't matter if a friend tells you to get in touch with Julia Roberts, Matt Damon or the head of the William Morris Agency. You are your own. Get that into your head before you even pack your suitcase. There are many people in this business of acting who are powerful and can't even get their own relatives or friends connected. It's not as easy as people think. The days of nepotism still exist, but even if you are very well connected, you must be ready to deliver if opportunity knocks. You can't just sit back and expect to be "hooked up".

And you can't sit back and expect your well-connected family or friends to protect you. YOU are on your own. I've known many people in this business. Some I've been happy to help and some I have not. The one's I've helped I knew could and would come through. To this day I will not recommend anyone unless I would hire that person myself. It works for me. Let's be hypothetical for a moment: Your mailman's wife's cousin (by marriage) knows someone at one of the major casting offices. By luck, your name comes up over dinner at a family gathering one evening, and low and behold you get an interview. STOP. Do not pass go, do not collect $200. Do not go out and buy a house, a Mercedes, a new wardrobe, and stay off the phone. You don't have a five-year television series yet. My business partner of 15 years, Al Onorato and I were in the position of auditioning some of those relatives 17 times removed. It did not help them read a script any better than if we met through the normal interview process. If you can get in the door, terrific, but remember, once you get in, you are on your own. Long before I started casting I needed a connection to get my career started again. My former boss at Universal, Roberta Ross, and then a Vice President and now retired, made a call to the head of the steno pool on my behalf. I knew I could deliver and so did Roberta. I had worked as Roberta's assistant while in college and I could type 85 words a minute. In preparation for college I took a speedwriting course (a practical tool to know if you are going to go through 8 years of lectures). In today's day and age, the laptop has replaced the steno pads. I was on track to being one of the leading script typists Universal Studios ever saw. Sure it was only typing scripts, which sucked in those days with only a typewriter, but I got in the door AND I delivered. From the steno pool, I moved up and eventually became an assistant in the casting department.

Let's go a bit further. You are a good friend of mine and I think that you are talented. I have a number of connections in town and I get you in to see the biggest producer in the city. I think that the role is perfect for you. You look right, you have the right height, hair color, etc. But—Can you act? Can you make that character believable? Do the words of the writer bring to life the character??

And, are you even ready to be in this office or any other office for work? If not, don't blame me. I got you the meeting. You just didn't cut it. Now hold on, don't toss this book in your nearest wastebasket. I did not infer that you were not a good enough actor for the role, you just didn't cut it. Your hairline could have been wrong for the role—I don't know. I did my best and got you the interview—I could not change your hairline and, when I got you the interview, I had no idea that the role was going to be cut of out the script. Don't despair. When I was the Director of Talent at Columbia Pictures Television, I was assigned a project that, to this day, I believe was one of my proudest pieces of casting. I brought in an actress whom I thought was dead perfect for the role. I couldn't have picked a better actress in age, look and ability. She ended up not getting the role because the producer thought that she had one "lazy" eye that would not photograph in a flattering way whatever that meant. I was disappointed, but in my optimistic tone said, "Not to worry, we'll find another actress." We recast the role and incidentally, the actress with the "lazy" eye hasn't stopped working since.

Casting is very subjective—what I see—you may not see—what you see, I may not see. There are too many variables involved in casting one role—and we will discuss in a later chapter. Getting back to the original point; before you cash in a favor (that means you make an acquaintance feel obligated to arrange for a meeting or audition) be certain that you can carry out your end of the deal. Make sure you know your material and whatever you do, don't drop your friend's name in hopes that based on that relationship; you'll be signing a contract on the spot. The good news is that you got in the door. You may be the world's greatest actor and your look might be totally wrong according to the casting director. Don't assume anything. Make the producer and director or casting director think that the image of the character should look just like you. Sell it with the acting and become what they are looking for. If all else fails, you have met another casting director and if you are a good actor, chances are good that you will return to that office at some time for another role.

Meeting with a casting director. My general interviews typically last for about twenty minutes; other casting directors take five. It is within this time that you can tell the casting director about yourself and your future goals. If you get a congenial casting director interviewing you, you may have the opportunity to break down some walls and discuss mutual interests. A good casting director will try to break the ice and make the actor feel as comfortable as possible. So an actor walks into my office and I invite him to sit down. I take his picture and resume (assuming he has one) and get an idea of where he is from and go from there.

"I see you've done some regional theater." I say. "Yes, back in Illinois." "How long have you been here?" "About a year and a half." The actor responds. "Well, are you making a living as an actor? Your resume doesn't list any other credits." "Well,

I'm a waiter at the Marina for the time being." "Oh—well, what classes are you enrolled in?" I ask. "I'm not in class, I'm sort of looking around for a good one."

This usually means that the actor reads the ads in the trade papers and never phones, or inquires whether or not he can audit a class, how much it costs, can he come in for an interview, etc. He is doing nothing to advance his profession. This is when my annoyance may show. Why do you call yourself an actor when you're not doing anything about acting? This is like saying you are a doctor, and just sitting at home glancing through the local drug store ads for Vitamins, just to see what's new in town.

"So you want to be an actor? Then act like one!" I say. An actor goes to classes, takes dance class, voice class, cold-reading class, dialect class—get into a theatre piece—It's very tiring to "beg" actors to hone their craft. And quite frankly, you just took 20 minutes of my time when someone who is clearly intent on getting into the profession of acting could have been sitting in your place.

Statistically, if you are good, you will be seen and given a shot. If you are not, then continue to study. Do not give up at this point in time. So many actors come to me at the point of suicide and say, "But I'm pounding the pavement, I seek work, I seek agents, I audition, I study I know I'm a good actor but I can't get a break." I sit listening, because I already know the pain of sitting in a steno pool for two long horrible years, knowing that I was creative and I only needed that "one break."

Make note of the next bullet and don't forget it. I will not be holding your hand if you do not listen and screw up (and even if you did listen still wouldn't hold your hand.)

NEVER EVER GO IN ON AN AUDITION THAT CALLS FOR A DIALECT UNLESS YOU ARE PROFICIENT IN THAT PARTICULAR ACCENT

My long time friend Nicholas Guest, a fine actor is also very accomplished dialectician. Casting Director's may always count of Nick if he physically fits the bill and must do any number of accents. Why? Because he studied until he got it right—and accents in his film, television and feature film work are a source of pride.

Agents trust you to be up front about your qualifications, and I trust the agent. So if you come in and give a crappy reading, with respect to the dialect, its' The Kiss of Death in my office.

You might as well tell me you are a proficient horseman and have never sat on a saddle in your entire life.

Which reminds me: When you are on an interview when you are trying to find an agent, don't be an idiot. Tell the agent what you can do, cannot do, will do and will not do. Al Onorato and I did a well-received Movie of the Week at Columbia Pictures Television in the early 80's we cast the wonderfully talented and sweet human being, the late Dana Hill (who would later become my friend and neighbor). Anyway, the project was called Fallen Angel, it was a sensational script by Lew Hunter, so wonderfully sweet, sensitive, and bold. It was the first Movie of the Week dealing with the subject of child pornography.

Another stroke of casting luck was in finding one of my favorite actors named Richard Masur. Yes, it is possible for casting directors to have favorite actors. "What does that have to do with anything?" you ask. Well, just because Richard is one of my favorite actors (I think I've worked with him twice in 20 years), if you have a favorite casting director, don't annoy them every time they get a project. While casting one of the teenage boys for the film, we found a wonderfully talented young 14 year-old.

When we phoned his agent to hire him, the agent called back to say that; "the parents were opposed to the subject matter based on their religious beliefs." Well, they are (as you are) totally entitled to rejecting a project that is not within their value system, integrity, morals etc. Now, had the 14 year old, or his parents, advised the agent about their religious concerns, it would be safe to say that the agent would have checked with the parent prior to submitting their client. Additionally, the actor and the parents read the script prior to the audition and the actor came in and auditioned anyway. Why not just be up front and "pass" after reading the material. I was working on an art film as a favor to one of my favorite legitimate and well-respected producers in town. There was a period of about 12 minutes in the mid to late 90's that soft, classy adult films were in, like Showtime's well-written series "Red shoe Diaries." Four different prominent female film directors were directing the script in four different countries—one from each respective country. Well, as luck might have it, three of the directors were joys to work with, but the lunatic from the United States (I can't say her name because you wouldn't believe it anyway) needed some actor who could "get fully aroused" on cue. "Do you know of any?" She asked me. "What am I—a frickin' sex psychic? I replied.

This nut case (otherwise referred to in our business as a loose canon) is asking me if I really know of someone who can get aroused in front of a set full of people. To make a long story short, I was so pissed off that I asked the producer to have the extra's casting director find someone. End of story. Now, I am not suggesting that you tell your agent whether or not you can get aroused on a set or not, but do let them know about your religious beliefs and ethics and whether or not you will do nudity or even soft nudity. Daytime soaps are notorious for t and a and within the last 10 years, the nighttime dramas go pretty far. Do not except roles that you will be uncomfortable with because, quite frankly—you will not do good work.

CHAPTER SEVEN

Scams-R-Us

I was speaking with an actor friend the other day who asked, hy are you schlepping around the country with your protecting the actor act"? 'Why, asked I?' Because it sickens me to read about, hear about or being asked about what are obvious scams in the acting community.

Yes, it is true that I am an actors advocate and life long educator and have always wanted to protect the actor. The actor one of the most vulnerable human beings walking around.

As a past President of the Casting Society of America, one of the issues on the Board table for over 5 years was the casting director teaching courses around town.

We are now in the year 2004 and the teaching guidelines have changed radically and drastically.

In the old days, casting directors were paid an honorarium of $50.00 to go to various workshops and teach cold reading courses. As the years rolled by, the acting classes have become more and more available, not only to actors, but in big bucks for the showcase or class producers. This is not to say that all of these workshop schools are scams. They are not. There is a list of recommended schools at the back of this book, which I personally know to be ethical and do provide the actors with solid coursework.

Here is the issue now is 2004. Are you going to class to meet a working casting director with hope of being hired? OR, are you going to class to learn how to cold read and audition? The answer has become obvious Casting directors have little time to give general interviews any longer and this is a way to see 20 or 30 actors and their work in an evening session.

What do I say in these situations? When I am on the teaching circuit, with my cold-reading and auditioning technique classes the first words out of my mouth are am here tonight as a teacher—not as a casting director. If you are here to get work on one of my projects, please leave. You are here to learn how to book, not only my projects, but also projects all over the city.

Yes, I agree, it's a good way to get to meet a working casting director, but if you are no ready to be out in the community booking work, please go into these courses with the objective of learning—not booking a job. Check the credentials of the instructor (casting director) and look on www.Imdb.com, watch the trade papers and the production reports to see who is casting and teaching and also which teachers are just teaching their respective courses and auditioning, interviewing, scene study, improvisation, etc. Network, ask friends or colleagues where they recommend studying.

Does the term teach mean the following to anyone reading this chapter?

1) To defend and protect the actor?
2) To share knowledge and life experience?
3) To share experiences and perhaps learn from each other?
4) To get your face in front of a casting director and hope that he or she will hire you?
5) To pay money to think that you might have a better shot at booking a job or at the least meeting a casting director.

The answer could be any or all of the above.

"To teach is to change a life forever". Anonymous.

I hold a Lifetime California Teaching Credential in Theatre Arts and have always thought that I was teaching so that the actor could learn. Process, choice making, auditioning technique and interviewing. That, in all honesty was the original goal of casting director/teachers. And then the issue came to the attention of the Casting g Society of America's Board of Directors.

For five years, we discussed, month after month, year after years, meeting after meeting. What ultimately came out of these meetings was an agreement with the Screen Actors Guild of America.

The agreement as it stands today is that Casting Director's who teach are not permitted to announce what show or projects they are casting. Additionally, a disclaimer is to be in all print, stating that the presence of a casting director is NOT a guarantee of work.

Be advised that I do NOT know every single teacher and coach around the country, but the respective Screen Actor's Guilds are very good sources of ethical coaches, teachers and coursework. Ask your fellow actors as well as doing your own research.

How do you recognize a scam? IF you are asked to pay for anything up front LEAVE IMMEDIATELY. The only one person whom your might leave a deposit with is a photographer, and the deposit goes to the photographer directly, not an agent, manager, promoter, company representing the photographer as part of a package.

CHAPTER EIGHT

The Catch 22 Syndrome

In all the years that I have been a casting director, another of the most common complaints I hear from aspiring young actors is I am in a Catch 22 situation. How do I get out of it?

First of all, let's define what is meant by a "catch 22 situation.

You want to act, but cannot get an agent. You cannot get an agent because you have never worked as an actor, have no tape or film on yourself and no one wants to take a chance on a total unknown.

Even if an agent took a chance on you and you were up for a role, you do not have your union card and the producer will not make it possible for you to get one. So you cannot get work because you have no credentials or your union card. You cannot get credentials or a union card because no one will hire you without either of them. Like a hamster running circles in a cage.

What to do?

The chapter upcoming deals specifically with how to find an agent, what to do about pictures and resumes, and how to get meetings with agents, personal managers and/or casting directors.

CHAPTER NINE

The All Important Agent

- - - - - -

On of my favorite personal friends as well as colleague Fern Champion just 'tells it like it is'...here is what Fern has to say:

"For starters, the difficulty...there are just far too many casting directors, making it more difficult. Now that I go that out of the way... the easier, there are so many more outlets this day in age that give actors chances to be seen. We have become so much more diversified with cable shows, web-series, independent films being recognized as main strea. Difficulty...it's not as much fun as it used to be. Used to be able to pick up the phone and enjoy conversations about not only our project, but about life. Now phones are obsolete with everything being done electronicall through mails and online breakdowns. A little cold. The personality ahs been taken out of the process between casting directors, agents and managers. Easier...there is much more talent available these days. The schools, coaches, workshops, all help our actors to become more equipeed and prepared...difficulty, finance has become much much less to casting director's because the abundance of us. Producers go shopping for the 'least expensive' – then they are sorry that money ahs become much less, when the work has become much harder. However, if I did not w=love wht I do, even if I didn't win last year's Emmy Award, it's still exciting, challenging and no day is ever the same. And besides, what else would I do that gives me the rush and the drive every day that I am in the game... Finding new actors is a thrill, nothing like it in the world...for me that is —and that ain't easy!!!!" Fern Champion.

Are you ready for an agent? Hold on—because this is the 21st century—perhaps the most difficult time in the history of show biz to find an agent who will believe in you. First of all, few agents will even see an actor unless they have tape (DVD) or have extensive theatre work. One just doesn't send a picture out and expect 100 representatives to pick up their phones and stand in line to meet with you. I have met thousands and thousands and thousands of actors over the years. I thought that was a bit exaggerated until I looked up some of Onorato/

Franks and Associates credits. On one show alone, Al and I put 6400 actors to work in 4 seasons of a courtroom drama (Superior Court).

Out of thousands of actors, including those whom I have assisted in cold reading or interview technique through the years, and any actor to whom I have asked the question "Are you ready for an agent?"—only 5 have told me that they were not ready.

This is comparable to saying—are you ready to become a surgeon?

Acting, like medicine is a profession—(that word again). Get it into your head—ACTING IS A PROFESSION. Would a hospital hire you as a surgeon if you had no experience or credentials? I think not. So why would someone represent you if you were not ready to go out in the field and book work? Do you have what it takes? Are you skilled? Do you have talent? Have you studied?

Have you done theatre? Have you done anything other than call yourself an actor? BE HONEST—BE HONEST

Do you have actor friends? Do you network and talk to your actor friends? Do you look at their headshots? Do you like what you see? Does the photo represent your friend the way you see him or her? What style of photo do you want? Let's talk about photographs. And let's talk about what goes hand in hand with photographs—the AGENT.

Over the last 30 years or so, I have lectured throughout the nation. I have conducted private showcases, college level courses of the university level, and countless lectures for hundreds of actors. The most commonly question asked of me by actors:

"How do I get an agent?"

Most of you reading this book will not be ready for an agent. For those of you who believe that you are prepared and ready, you will learn some lessons about agents. The agent/actor relationship is rarely understood.

Again, let me point out that acting is a business. To be successful with this profession one must hire an agent and/or personal manager who can be trusted.

Not only trusted, but does this representative believe in you?

Are you ready to read in front of a top feature film casting director in the city? Are you ready to go out on a pilot audition (a pilot is the "trial" production of a proposal show for a network), which might land you a role for 5 or more years and make you a household name?

When I was an agent I would ask myself a series of questions:

Does this actor have what it takes? Is he/she skilled? Does he have talent? Has she studied? Has he done theatre? Has he done anything other than called himself an "actor?"

If an agent believes that you have "the look" then your chances are better in securing this representative. Agents are very subjective. I may think that you have "the look" but someone down the street might disagree. This is one of the reasons that there are so many agency and personal management companies.

So in answer to "How do I get an agent?" I say, "Be prepared or get prepared."

So if an agent believes that you have the look, then what happens? Can you deliver?

There is a wonderful agent (now personal manager) in town I know named Tom Korman. Some of us in the casting community refer fondly to Tom as "The Pizza Man—he delivers." Tom is a terrific guy and a terrific agent. I don't think that there was ever a time when he didn't send me the most well suited actors. Tall, short, thin, large, stars, stars to be, no names, whatever—whomever Tom sent to casting directors was an actor ready to work before the camera. So when I ask you to think carefully about whether or not you are ready for an agent or personal manager, be very honest with yourself. You need to know if you are able to walk into a casting director's office, book a job, AND make you agent and/or personal manager look good." Holy $#!@—You mean to tell me that's how agents become famous? Because of the actor? Damn straight! Don't be a jerk.

For those of you planning to go into television, you better know who Steve is and what he has done for TV)! (See www.Imdb.com).At any rate, the bottom line remains that if you want to get a good agent, you have to be able to deliver and get work. The bigger, larger, and more powerful agents must book a percentage of their salary or they are out of a job! If they are paid $150,000 a year, then they are expected to bring in to the agency about 3 times that amount. Pressure? You want pressure? The head of an agency must keep control over costs, salaries and other CEO stuff. The agents beneath the CEO must find lucrative clients. Below them is you, the client, who must be able to get into a room full of people and book a job. If you believe you can handle this, then go ahead and start submitting your photo and resume.

In this particular time in film and television, it is very difficult to secure an agent or personal manager. Why? The influx of actors is enormous. And more coming up the ranks. The good news is the percentage of actors who can really deliver for the agent is very small. If you know in your heart that you are ready to work, then try securing an agent. How? Be seen in theatre, be seen in daytime, be seen, do bulk mailings and if at all possible start collecting tape of your work.

The Actor's Resume One of the most essential tools in your quest for an acting career is your resume. Before we enough discuss the piece of paper, called the resume, which conveys something about you, make note of the following:

First of all, don't lie. Don't fudge and don't fabricate. Remember everyone had to have their first recognition at some point in their lives. You should use all education, regardless of whether or not you graduated from a university program or theatre training, dance, voice etc. If you speak more than one language, list them Many might disagree, but I suggest that you put your height, weight, eye color, and hair color on your resume

My good friend and colleague Mike Fenton (Founder, C.S.A.) suggests putting the date of the photo on your resume as well. I think that is a great idea. The photo you walk in with is the photo that looks like you NOW— not ten years ago. When the time comes to take a new shot—go for it. The photo you are currently using could serve you well for two or three years.

Make certain your resume has a contact number, both on the resume and on the back of the photo. (See example of resume in back of book) If your resume gets separated from your photo, make certain the casting director knows how to reach you. If you speak in dialects, state which ones. E.g. Polish, English, Latin and even sign-language.

Make certain that you list all important "special skills" at the bottom of the resume and IF you speak languages, list them as a 'special skill'.

CHAPTER TEN

The Five Minutes In The Casting Director's Office

Here is a commonly asked question I get as a casting director:

"What do you most dislike when an actor walks into your office for a general interview and/or reading?"

I don't like attitude and I don't like an actor walking in with coffee or a drink in his hand and I don't like if an actor is unprepared. E.g. no picture or resume and isn't prepared for the meeting or reading and please never bring props into a meeting or reading in my office.

More explanation:

There are several things that an actor does in a general reading that distresses me. The thing that bothers me the most is when an actor cops an attitude. When I say attitude, I mean that he she is trying to be something they're not. The old chip on the shoulder should be avoided at all costs. This is the attitude that says to me that, "This actor believes that he needs no acting lessons, needs no direction and could go out and teach other actors a thing or two." I immediately go into the psychology portion of my brain, which tells me that there is a big mass of insecurity sitting in front of me.

Why is this actor so insecure? What is the low self-esteem all about? Where is this tremendous recognition need coming from?

What are all their fears?

One thing that I do find acceptable is when an actor wishes to enter a reading in character and go directly into the scene with no "chit chat" and introduction proceeding. If you choose to use this method you must make this clear to the casting director or let the casting assistant know that this is your option. The casting assistant will let the casting director have this information before you enter the room. Typically when an actor enters for a reading, he is introduced to the producer and the director, then we would talk for a few minutes, ask the actor if he had any questions, and then proceed with the reading. The "chit chat" portion of this audition would be done after the initial reading. My experience has been that everyone and their dog feel that they are ready to get an agent or personal manager before their 8 x 10s have dried.

CHAPTER ELEVEN

Photographs

Your major calling card along with your talent is your photograph. Overzealous actors will try anything to be noticed.

There once was a guy who climbed through my window at MGM. It got my attention, but I would be more impressed by an accurate looking headshot rather than some random guy leaping through my window like Superman!

If you are wondering how much you should spend on headshots

I will say from $100 per roll to $300 per roll including makeup and hair. Prices will very from state to state. Personally, I would not spend more than $300.00. Check the photographer's portfolio before making the decision to hire him.

All you need is a good black and white headshot, nothing fancy.

You want a normal looking photo that looks like you, not what you want to look like. To find a good photographer I advise to speak to your actor friends. Look at their headshots and if you like what you see, get the photographers information.

Every photographer in town has samples (portfolios) of their work. Many advertise and state their prices. If they do not advertise their prices, call them and discuss pricing with them.

And before you commit, study their portfolios and make sure you like and trust the photographer. If you don't feel comfortable, I suggest that you find another photographer. Also, don't go seeking out a photographer if you are not having a good day or just had a fight with your significant other (or both for that matter). Be in a good receptive mood and use your instinct like you would use you instinct when making acting choices.

Will you relax with this photographer—will he/she get from you the look that best represents YOU? When you are finished wi the shoot you will get a proof back usually in a matter of two days. Typically, when you see your headshot you will scream about how much you hate them, how much you hate the photographer and how much he/she screwed you financially.

Only recently have I really been unhappy about my headshots.

First of all, I am overweight at this point in my life, I'm not happy with my skin and my dermatologist said that I could repair the skin if I went back 30 years and stayed out of the sun.

Face-lifts aren't my thing, plus at my age and being overweight there is a lot more that needs lifting than just my face. But there is a difference. I don't care because my photo is not my calling card. Your photo, on the other hand, is part of your calling card.

My advice is to find 3 to 5 people, friends, agent, and personal manager and maybe even the photographer. Do not let your family choose your headshot and by all means do not, under any circumstance, choose your own headshot. Get opinions and keep score—the highest number of points is the shot you should go with. A casting director, agent and personal manager are looking for a headshot that looks like you. Don walk into a hair salon and ask them to make you look like Sharon Stone. You may ask for a Sharon Stone look, but remember, you look like you, not Sharon Stone, not Leonardo de Caprio, but you. Many actors ask me what I look for in a photo. I look to see what comes out of the photo's eyes, your eyes, and I go strictly by instinct. An actor asked me if I looked at the resume first before I take a chance on bringing an actor in. Yes, of course I look at the resume. If I sense that the actor is serious and I feel that this might be a gem, I certainly try to meet the person. While we are on the subject of headshots—ONE/maybe TWO—not 30 headshots representing different moods. A photo that looks like you—period—that's all—not a oil portrait, in color, not framed ust a black and white, 8 x 10 photo—PLEASE—trust me.

Photos are expensive—they should represent you for a good year and maybe two—if you lose an ear from one photo shoot to another—have another shoot done immediately. Otherwise— leave well enough alone. "Well, I like to show the casting director my range." Range, schmange—A straight headshot and a comical (or light) shot, that's it. We are not including commercial or print shots. If you are not going after comedy, then just one straight shot will do. If you are a character actor, do not try to look glamorous. Every photographer in town, as I have stated has a portfolio. If they don't have a portfolio—you shouldn't be in their studio. Within the portfolio is a sample of their work. Some photographer's work is displayed. TVI in Los Angeles and New York schools, have many, many photographers work prominently displayed in their reception areas. Do some research. Look in Backstage/Dramalogue and do some research.

Many photographers advertise and will state their prices— otherwise, phone and discuss costs with them. Meet the photographer before you hire him/her for a photo shot. If you don't feel comfortable and at east—keep looking. My own favorite photographer, George Hurrell—now deceased is represented by my good friend and gifted actor Allen Rich.

Allen represents Mr. Hurrell work and in the mid 80'sI had an opportunity to have Mr. Hurrell photograph me—for the sum of $5,000 (a bargain) but even I am not vain enough to pay $5,000 for a photo session. Listen to me—all you need is a black and white head shot, not a glamorous George Hurrel portrait *1—a good shot that looks like you—not what you want to look like. Have I made my point? The second most commonly asked questions asked by actors is "What do you look for in a photo?"

What do I, Jerry look for? What do the eyes convey?

An actor asked me if I looked at the resume first before I take a chance on bringing an actor in. Yes, of course I look at the resume. If I sense that the actor is serious and I feel that this might be a gem, I certainly try to meet the person. While we are on the subject of headshots—ONE/ maybe TWO—not 30 headshots representing different moods. A photo that looks like you—period—that's all it doesn't have to be in color, not framed—a black and white, 8 x 10 photo—PLEASE—trust me.

*Color for print work and/or modeling 'zed' cards.

Photos are expensive—they should represent you for a good year and maybe two—if you lose an ear from one photo shoot to another—have another shoot done immediately. Otherwise— leave well enough alone. "Well, I like to show the casting director my range." Range, schmange—A straight headshot and a comical (or light) shot, that's it. We are not including commercial or print shots. If you are not going after comedy, then just one straight shot will do. If you are a character actor, do not try to look glamorous. Every photographer in town, as I have stated has a portfolio. If they don't have a portfolio—you shouldn't be in their studio. Within the portfolio is a sample of their work.

With respect to color shots—they are recommended for "online" photos—particularly if you have red hair, blue, green eyes, etc.—Modeling and print shots are acceptable in color— otherwise, just stick with the black and white photos.

Remember, you can post your photo on many websites – I strongly recommend Actor's Access which is a branch of Breakdown Services.

CHAPTER TWELVE

Daytime Tv – A Great Learning Experience

I have always been a major fan of actors from daytime (soap operas). Think about the discipline of learning a new script every night for the next day taping. It would be comparable to doing a new play on Broadway, every evening for 5 nights.

One of my closest friends as well as colleagues is Mark Teschner. Mark has been casting "General Hospital" since 1989. His taste, instinct and eye for talent have garnered him countless ARTIOS (CSA Awards) as well as six Emmy Awards for daytime casting.

I asked Mark for his take on today's actor entering daytime. Here is what he had to say.

"My advice to any young actor is to do it for the love of acting, the respect for the craft can't be about that. Study acting, become the best actor you can be, so when you get that elusive audition you are able to deliver.

If you are not getting audition, then you need to create opportunity, even if it means making a short film or creating a web series. Don't wait… create."

I would like to add what Mark suggest. If a short film is not feasible there are countless number of theatre events happening daily. Find a play. Get a classroom of students and assign "showcase" productions.

CHAPTER TWELVE-DAYTIME TV A GREAT LEARNING EXPERIENCE

Note that this is the second chapter on daytime. I stress daytime because of the large number of actors who have branched out from daytime to nighttime, to Emmy Awards as well as Oscars.

In the early days of television, and through the early 80's, prior to "Luke and Laura" (General Hospital) becoming one of daytimes most recognized and popular characters, actors looked down on daytime. Why? I guess ego – Actor's felt that feature films were the optimal goal and if all else failed, a starring role in a night time drama. Sit-coms were big and getting bigger. I recall Jay Leno sitting in my office and discussing a career in acting. Becoming a "more than an acquaintance" as the years went by – I showed him his head shot and the notes I had written on his resume. "Very prominent jaw – would work as good character, but not leading man." Well, I guess I was correct. I admire Jay Leno because he is as nice a guy as he was in the late 70's – approachable – normal – happy – and having just recently left the Tonight Show – I sense on to bigger and better. It's true that nice guys do win out.

Gloria Monty (Executive Producer) of 'General Hospital' – it is said "saved ABC from bankruptcy with her taste in talent and creative juices in writing.

In all of the years that we knew each other (we are both from the same town in New Jersey)we had only one disagreement. When the search was on for the character of _____there were three or four casting director's on a 'search.' The late Marvin Paige, Sally Powers, Alo and I as ABC consultants.

It was Sally Powers who brought in Demi Moore and when I went into the waiting room to meet and greet and try to put the actresses at ease – Demi's eye's popped right out at me – I said hello, and with this smokey voice was very gracious. I walked back into Gloria's office and announced "there is an actress in the waiting room who is "_____". Oh, please let her be able to act. I arranged that Demi would be interviewed and read as the 5th out of 10 actresses. I recall that Sally Powers read with Demi and both her eyes and my eyes welled up. Demi WAS "_____". Gloria didn't want to see any other actresses, but being the class act that she was, we saw the rest of the candidates and when Emma Samms walked in, I suggested to Gloria that we read her for a different role. Gloria agreed and we put her on tape as a prospective candidate. When we viewed the tape, Gloria said – "Oh, Jerry, much much too young." – Gloria, please change her hairdo, put her in a black dress and I know she can pull this off.

It costs money to 'test' actor's. The cameraman as well as entire crew stay after a regular day of taping and we begin to tape candidates for potentital roles. "I would only do this for you Jerry – I'm way over budget. New York fell in love with Emma Samms and she went on to nighttime and stardom in those days working with Aaron Spelling on one of his nighttime hits.

This story goes back to what I have alluded several times throughout my book. It is never ONE person who makes a career for someone. An agent or personal manager get an actor seen by a casting director, the casting director takes the actor to the producer and director and the powers that be and that actor books the role that was meant for him/her.

I ran into George Clooney at the supermarket one evening. "Jere – if you want a pilot to fail, just put ME in it." George, don't be so negative. When you lose your pretty boy looks and become the leading man in a few years, you'll hit – and probably be a star." – Do you know where I can find marshmellows?

I love Clooney – he hit big on _____a show which NBC executives turned down – however my pal Lori Openden stood up in the screening room and told the execs that they were crazy – "she" saw a major hit. And so it was that _____became a major hit and Clooney was off and running.

I can't remember whether or not I mentioned keeping notes when you meet a casting director. Yes, we do remember actors – and yes, we do bring the same actor in frequently until the right role is owned by them.

Bryan Cranston – 5 time Emmy Winner and Golden Globe winner for "Breaking Bad" I have known since the 70's. Bryan came into our office numerous times, but not until a role in "Chips" did he earn his SAG card – and we worked together several times after. It was Bryan's personal manager who reminded me that Bryan was available, I took Bryan to the producer who took Bryan to the director and there you have it – another member of the prestigious Screen Actor's Guild.

Tenacity is a key adjective here — you have got to hang in and trust your representative. No rep, then mail — do NOT drop off into casting director's offices. Get onto Actor's Access where casting director's can view your face and resume within seconds. Make the rounds — to the post office. Casting director's are so busy casting the next episode in tv — there is no time — ever for the lost "general interviews."

Yes, we all become discouraged, but, serving in protocol at the White House, I learned my most valuable lesson. "Always come in on a positive." Somewhere in the back of my mind, I think my friend Ronald told me that 30 years ago.

Leave your ego outside of the office, be yourself, ask questions and do the best you can do — which to me is following your instinct for a character. If the director wants to adjust you, he will let you know.

The kiss of death is asking to read for another role while in the office. Let your agent make the suggestion to a casting director. C.D.'s have ego.'s — It shouldn't be the actor's idea, it should be the director's or c.d.'s idea. (Remember my actress friend Pricilla Barnes whom the director didn't care for — thus — I asked her to put a dark wig on and change outfits, I taped her and she booked the role — with a pseudonym. It will happen for you when the role is right and your are right for the role.

As I mentioned above, daytime soap opera work was looked down upon by many actors. There was an element of snobbiness attached to soap opera acting even though soap operas have always been a part of the mass media. The soap operas began on radio and some converted to television and some have never left.

I mentioned my friend, the late Gloria Monty,

Executive producer of General Hospital. As the story is told in the early 80's, it was Gloria's brilliant vision, which kept ABC in business. The soap opera world on ABC and in particular General Hospital brought in countless millions of dollars to the network and literally kept them afloat.

Fortunately for us, Alo and I were West Coast Consultants to Daytime for three years and also we oversaw NBC's daytime drama Days of Our Lives. I I personally enjoy casting Daytime more than any other area of casting. Why? I feel and have always felt that Daytime Drama affords an actor a great break in learning acting, staging, movement, a new play a day. The crossover (leaving one medium and going into another e.g. being seen on TV. and being discovered for a role in feature films equals crossover) is one of the, if not the best way to make it from tv to film.

Actors constantly ask if they should do daytime? Well, obviously.

The learning, the exposure is incredible. Why am I so strong on my belief that an actor should do a soap opera? Several reasons the training as I have said is extraordinary is the discipline: it is as good as the theatre; you get paid and get free education: try it out if you have the following points in our favor:

1) You can act
2) You are nice to look at
3) You're in good physical shape
4) You have sizzel (sex appeal)
5) You have a slight edge to go along with the sizzle

You need to submit your picture and resume to any and all daytime (soap opera) casting directors in Los Angeles or New York, regardless of whether or not you have representation.

Ironically, it seems that casting directors like Mark Teschner,

Daytime's leading Casting Director—currently on a long success with General Hospital, Jackie Briskey of Passions, Fran Bascom,

Days of Our Lives, love finding new faces who can act.

Actors do make the crossover and go on to greater success.

I mentioned earlier that I have been quoted as saying "give me a New York actor any day of the week." Doing a daytime show is literally learning a new "play" every night. New York actor's study hard and then you have the three threat actors like _____as well as "Doogie Houser's"----------------------

Meg Ryan, Alex Baldwin, Joe Lando, David Hasselhoff, on and on— the daytime world is a phenomenal starting ground for any actor or actress. And the casting directors really have the finest in taste.

I am proud to have worked with Gloria Monty of General Hospital fame and John Conboy of The Young and the Restless, as well as Betty Corday and her son Ken, creator of "Days of Our Lives."

Capitol and most recently Guiding Light. We have had great times together through the years, nurturing and guiding a bevy of actors, including Emma Samms and Demi Moore.

If you are going to try daytime, either through your representative or through yourself, be honest on your resume.

Everyone has to start somewhere and the Daytime Casting Directors have keen eyes and great instinct when looking at headshots…. repeat— your photo should look just like you. No body shots are necessary at this point in the game, but keep yourselves in good soap shape.

Watch the daytime dramas to get a sense of each storyline on ABC, CBC, NBC, cable and observe the actors: look at the faces and look at the theme of the show—. Do some research. Look in Backstage to find photographers who advertise and will state their prices: otherwise, phone and discuss costs with them.

Meet the photographer before you hire him/her for a photo shot. If you don't feel comfortable and at ease, keep looking.

Many original soap dramas have gone by the wayside, however, nighttime has a "plethora" of dramas, not unlike daytime. Continuing story lines with ensemble cast. ENSEMBLE cast – a key word for success. Can you imagine anyone other than the actors on "Seinfeld", "Cheers", Mary Tyler Moore"-------

-------being played by any other actor? That is the greatest compliment to casting.

My colleague and friend April Webster was deemed "brilliant" by writer/producer/director J.J. Abrams. Yes, I think she is brilliant in her imagination. Can you think of any other actor on "Lost" or "Criminal Minds" or _____being played by any other actor? This is why April has a bountiful of awards and is one of the most beloved casting directors in our industry. She is what the Casting Society of America has always strived for: good taste and "actor" friendly casting directors.

First cardinal rule: ALWAYS have available, a picture and resume with you at all times. General Interviews (very few and far between these days) 1) be yourself 2) make certain that you have picture and resume with you/or portfolio when Requested (keep some in the trunk of your car) and make use of the internet highway.

Breakdown Services, the most ethical bible of the industry is a must. Pay a modest fee to join "Actor's Access" – pay a modest fee to join EXPLORE talent – one never knows who will see your photo.

I just finished casting a film in Roanoke, Virginia. Where did 98% of the actors come from? I found them on EXPLORE talent as well as Actor's Access.

3) wear appropriate attire—no breasts hanging out and no tight blue jeans revealing a man's shortcomings

4) never touch the casting director accept to shake hands

5) if you don't have the credentials to back yourself up, then don't lie

6) do not reveal your age to a casting director (see your SAG rulings)

7) leave your ego outside of the office as well as your personal problems. Don't enter an audition with a chip on your shoulder because your girlfriend cheated on you – deal with that later on – AFTER your interview. Focus, be clear on what the director wants from the character, and yes, it is appropriate to ask questions – don't make it 20 questions, ask about the "character's" attitude, likeability, does the actor have an edge? Yes, if you are going for a high drama – you must have an edge along with the other "moods" that any character calls for.

8) use your eyes

9) be yourself

10) be yourself

11) be yourself—don't try to convince a casting director how wonderful you are.

CHAPTER THIRTEEN

Over Forty And Holding

Dear Casting Director: I'm forty five years old and I have been out of the business for many years—raising a family, finishing school, career change, etc. how long should I try to get back to acting? Dear person: First of all, were you a working actor prior to your "taking a hiatus" or were you calling yourself an actor and not even taking class? Or do you have credential to lean on from years ago. My answer is quite simple. If you wake up at 50, having struggled to make it as an actor, and you are barely making a living, I think you may wish to consider a backup profession. I met with an actor and his father with respect to the 20 year old's career. The guy will probably make it big—with his look, sense of humor and dedication to studying.

CHAPTER FOURTEEN

I Lost My Job—My Career Is Over

Here is a scenario: Your agent calls and says that there is a role in a feature film being cast playing the sibling to Robert Redford,

Paul Newman, or Brad Pitt. You are perfect for the third or fourth lead and you must get to 20th Century Fox immediately to meet the casting director.

You break your neck trying to find something to wear, cut yourself shaving (face or legs), trip over a chair and break your little toe in your mania, and are made aware that your car battery is dead. You decide to grab a cab and go to the audition.

You arrive at the audition and look at the script (or in some cases you have the opportunity of taking the script with you to study for some allocated time period) and begin preparing for the big moment the reading.

According to the Screen Actors Guild contract, an actor is permitted to see a full script 24 hours prior to a reading or meeting. AND, if a script is not available to be taken out of a casting director's office—it is available at the office to read. So now you have calmed yourself down and you know that this is the role that was sent to you from God above. You walk in the door and your heart starts sending the blood pumping through your brain "This is it! This is it!" screams your brain. Houses, limos, clothes, money, what you want could be yours. Before you open up your mouth you are picturing yourself in a new Mercedes. You go in and give what you consider to be the most amazing reading of your life and you leave exhilarated.

Days pass. Wine, drugs, sleepless nights, hundreds of phone calls to your friends telling them about the good news. Fantasy time.

Then the phone finally rings You are not rich and famous yet, which means that you have not hired your butler, and therefore must pick up the phone with your own two little hands. You pick it up and it's your agent. Sam Schmuck. Like a foghorn in your ear your agent says, "I just spoke with so and so and they thought that the reading was fabulous. Your look is sensational.

While this chatter is going on you are thinking, "Money,

European weekend. Mercedes . . ." While you are NOT listening, the agent continues—"but you didn't get the job because you are Caucasian and the writer just decided to make this character African American. You felt so heartbroken you just tuned out the rest of the conversation.

At this point in time, you hang up the phone and you start thinking about a) killing yourself; b) getting out of the business; c) phoning the producer and begging profusely; or d) all of the above.

You honestly believe that your career is over and that you will never work again. Let us stop for a moment and take a look at this situation. First of all, get a grip. This is only one role that you did not book. There will be many more opportunities—IF you keep up with your profession. You have to get into your head that this is a business. Whether it is a budget problem, you have the wrong look, your acting was not on the mark, whatever it may be at that moment, not getting the part is not the end of the world. Remember confidence and everything that goes with it is vitally important. Use it and do not get yourself down.

Don't be arrogant and cocky—that is not the message here. Be realistic.

CHAPTER FIFTEEN

"Say Goodnight Gracie" .....George Burns

Anyone going into comedy knows the expression—or they should know the expression "Say goodnight Gracie". If you don't, then get your ass to the library or on the computer and do some research on the great comedians of the 19th and 20th century. After you have finished reading with a casting director and they say, "Well, we'll see what happens" or "Gee, nice reading, we'll be in touch," do not start nagging them OR your agent OR your personal manager. And don't pressure someone who may have helped you get the appointment to begin with.

"Have you heard from Jerry's office yet?" "Do I have the job?"

"When will I know?" "Was I good?" "What did he say?" "Did he like me?" "Can I read it again?"

Get over yourselves! I'm sorry to say, but once you and the other 20 or 30 people I have seen that day leave my office, I don't think about you until the end of the day and perhaps two days—after I read my own notes and review the entire session.

AND—when you are finished with the reading and/or meeting—be gracious and leave the office. Years ago, I had a general interview with a new actor sent to me by one of my trusted agent colleagues. After a 20 minute or so meeting, I got up to shake the guy's hand—he in turn, slapped me on the back and said "So, Jer, let's get together for a beer sometime". Well, first of all—only my friends call me Jer. Everyone else is to refer to me as "Your Highness". And secondly—the last thing I want to do in my free time is having a beer with someone I've met for 20 minutes. As difficult as it is for an actor to understand, casting directors have lives outside of the office. Our off time is precious—we have families—we have close friends—and barely enough time to spend with them. So, please I've get social with a casting director. This is a business, not a social gathering.

I have had several questions asked recently by new actors whom I've met through the college speaking tour. These are the actors who always ask: "Is it true that this . . . . is it true that THAT happened? etc. etc. Don't ask me—I have been deemed the "Fort Knox of Hollywood" Don't kiss and tell—have some class.

Why is it that five actors leave my office and if they were to be interviewed by a network newscaster in my parking lot, they would all tell the newscaster that they just booked the job?

When I was starting out in the business, I let my entire circle of close friends know what was going on in my career. The mistake then, that I know now, is that I too was a gossip!

Keep your big mouths shut until your agent phones you and says "Hello actor, you booked the job with casting director Joe."

First of all, don't take power out of the moment. Give that to yourself. It will give you confidence to get the job done properly.

We all have been embarrassed at some time in our life when we thought that a job had been booked, and it falls through later on. In the meantime, you have called everyone you possible know to tell them that you got a job.

Have some class. Don't be a gossip . I have many friends who are actors. Some stars, some working steadily, some are just day players and some are superstars, and they all made the same mistake of "running their mouths." Out of excitement and pride, we want everyone to share the joy we get 'when' and 'if' we book an acting job.

Keep your professional life to yourself and to those closest to you. Hang with the people, and network with those people who support you the most, not suck you dry of your enthusiasm.

CHAPTER SIXTEEN

A Gift From God

One of the questions most frequently asked of me is do I believe that anyone can become an actor. No, I do not. In my most honest appraisal and opinion, I can suggest that there is the very select small group of "gifted" actors—or sometimes referred to as a natural actor.

Alo and I were casting a terrific independent feature film script called "Tree house" which unfortunately went nowhere. Sadly, the producer died and the film idea died with him.

The good news is that we met some terrific young actors in the casting process, one being Leonardo DiCaprio. Leonardo DiCaprio sat in our waiting room with his very cordial Dad waiting for his appointment time to read. We were running late that afternoon and I went into our reception area to apologize to the actors for our tardiness. When I returned to my office to join Alo, I remember saying, "Al, there's a kid out there with great energy and a terrific look—let's pray he can act".

When Leonardo entered my office—his energy was immediate and his grace and dignity for a young man were impressive. Then he opened his mouth to read one line from his 'side'. (part of a script) Al and I looked at each other and knew that this kid would get the lead role AND, after later in reviewing the day, we both agreed that Leo was destined for stardom. He had every quality physically, spiritually, and instinct of a blessed and gifted actor.

Directly after the reading, I went one step further and escorted Leonardo out of my office and asked to speak with his father. This is the first and only time I've ever done this.

The three of us moved out into the hallway for some privacy.

Right in front of Leo, I suggested to his Dad to" be careful with this boy's career—he was destined for stardom. Please have Leo make good choices in material as well as representatives". Leo "trust your own instincts and continue to hone your gift". I often wonder if Mr. DiCaprio believed me? I am very proud of Leo and his gifts—and prouder of his humbleness, kindness and his moral fiber.

I look toward actors like I look to great artists, great voices, and great gifted people. Streisand, Beverly Sills, Richard Burton,

Pavarotti, Josh Groban, Jack Nicholson are gifted. I say they have been "touched". Touched by whatever one believes in as a Higher Power. I feel that greatness in any area—politics, the arts, music, and particularly acting is not in our realm—no teacher or coach or "connection" to people of power in any profession can create "a gift". The two people to whom I have dedicated this book—

Renee Valente and Ron Meyer are both "gifted" and "annointed by the finger of a Higher Power". Renee is gifted with great instinct, an engaging persona, diplomacy of a statesman along with great moral fiber and—generosity of spirit to everyone she meets. My great friend Ron, next to my own brother, whom I hold in the highest esteem, is the most loyal man I know, with integrity and other intrinsic qualities that I have through my career tried to emulate. Loyalty in life is a very important and a rare quality. I am humbled and honored to call them friends in the truest sense of the word.

The fact that not everyone is fortunate enough to be given a "gift" is certainly not to scare anyone away from their dream— and particularly you who wish to become actors—just keep it in perspective. Some of you may become very active working actors for your entire career—some of you will change your minds and go into other professions and strive for other goals. Then there are perhaps those few of you who will let me know some day that perhaps you have read my book or heard me speak. If I can protect just one of you from major disappointment and conversely help just one of you to "make it"—remember—you are a 'chosen' one—so take your gifts and share them as long as you can breathe. And—keep your egos intact.

I've always believed that some of the mot talented people come from the regional areas of the country Regional theatre have some of the best actors around. Will we know them? Doubtful. These actors Opt to stay in the safe environment in which they were raised – our loss – but, keep your eyes wide open. We all know 'anointed' people. How can we help them? Support them, be positive,

Don't compare, hold no grudges and become familiar with the "optimist's creed" which states: "Be just As enthusiastic of others success as you are of your own.

The first rule for the actor at your level—is—"do not expect to be signed by a major agency like the most familiar names—

WILLIAM MORRIS, ICM, UNITED TALENT AGENCY,

CREATIVE ARTISTS AGENCY—you do not have the chops as yet. What you "might" have is the look. That is a totally different chapter (see comments in chapter "IT") The major agencies are no longer grooming their young clients as they did for many years. When I began in the business in 1964, the Contract Player program was still in existence at Universal City Studios. In 1968, Renee Valente, then Vice President of Talent and Casting for Columbia Television (formerly Screen Gems) started the Columbia Talent Program. These programs were similar to the original MGM and Warner Brothers contract player programs. Contract programs no longer exist. You are on your own to find your own coaches, teachers, mentors, agents, personal managers, and your trusted confidants.

CHAPTER SEVENTEEN

The Casting Couch Syndrome

One of the biggest jokes perpetrated on the entertainment industry is whether or not the "casting couch" exists. For those of you who are like me and look at the world through rose-colored glasses, let me tell you exactly what the "casting couch" is. The "casting couch" method of obtaining a job by paying favors to a producer, director, casting director or anyone connected to the business in order to get in introduction, meeting, or job with some VIP in the business. The "favor" I am referring to, is not running out to pick up laundry or to walk the dog, but rather the favor holds a more sexual connotation. When I was younger,

I was reticent to even consider the idea that someone would sleep around in order to get a job. I thought that people who do this could not possibly exist. Obviously they do, but you must continue to read in order to get the details. If in fact, the "casting couch" does exist, how do you get away from the stigma that if one gets a big break, they will falsely be labeled as "sleeping their way to that position. "The "casting couch" began with one of the heads of Warner Brothers studios back in the early days (1920's or so). Jack Warner, owner of the studios, had an eye for beautiful women and was in the position of "helping" these women get a start in the movie business. So, women would sleep with him, he would get them an extra job, and that would be the end of it.

Have I ever been aware of the "casting couch" syndrome? Yes, I have as a matter of fact. Many times. Originally, when Alo and I were in business together for so many years, it seemed that two or three of the same producers would frequently phone us to meet an actress they had discovered. Typically, these discoveries couldn't walk and chew gum at the same time, but nevertheless we accommodated these producers—only because they were our bosses. I hasten to add that our respect for these guys was little!

On one occasion in my early days when I was a casting assistant, one of my casting director supervisors was notorious for "helping" young girls. "Hi guys, this is John Doe, would you mind seeing this new actress for me?" Well, Alo and I laughed because we knew "John Doe" was getting some action. It was very annoying to have to bump another appointment to help pay favors back to people asking us to see their "squeeze of the week." The other time I saw the casting couch in action was when I was on location in Mississippi and my hotel room was across the hall from the director's. That director got more massages in one week than I got in a year! And—he was married.

Shame on him. The "casting couch" does not exist anymore. I do wish to state that on occasions in the last 20 years or so, every time I've sat on a panel or have been asked for an opinion of the casting couch, I must say that the term has primarily been associated with a producer or director. "Why not casting directors?" You ask.

The bank of talent today is comprised of thousands of members of the Screen Actors Guild. There are 30,000-35,000 members of AFTRA and then there are new and up-and-coming actors and middle-aged actors who are still trying to make it. Do you think that any casting director in their right mind would present an actor to a producer and director when the casting director knows that the actor can't act? With the egos in the city of Hollywood, a casting director would have to be a real idiot to take a chance like that. The competition in the casting and directing world today is just as competitive as it is in the actor's world. Casting Directors must now interview for assignments.

One would have to be a real yahoo to risk losing their job by bringing in unqualified actors, and usually without a SAG (Union) card. If you think you are going to get there fast by paying favors to a producer, director, casting director or anyone else who is connected, you're wrong! I sat back and shook my head when a franchised agent was indicted in 1995 for "having sex with a minor" and various other charges. What actor in their right mind would go on an interview to an agent's house or anyone's house after normal working hours? This is how you know if an actor is professional or not. Who, with any sanity, would go to an interview at a stranger's house? Are you people nuts? Get a grip. If you think that the "casting couch" does exist and you believe that it can help you—get out of this business right now—it will never happen that way. Earn your roles because you are right for the role and you can carry the acting— you have trained and are ready—you will sleep better at night and always be proud of whatever job you get—by virtue of the fact that you deserve it because you earned it through hard work and professionalism.

CHAPTER EIGHTEEN

Please Don't Tell Me Your Problems

— — — — — —

I have heard so many excuses from actors being late for given appointment times, or worse yet, not showing up at all to an audition or meeting. It's one thing to be late for a casting call, but showing up late on the set is a real no no. I'm not certain whether or not the actor is aware that for each minute they are late and may be holding up production, thousands of dollars are being thrown out the window. Be a pro and get to your appointment or call time 15-30 minutes early. Excuses: my car battery died and that's why I was late. Death in the family. The kid was sick and there was no babysitter available My dog got hit by a truck and I had to go home and tell the kids.

Actors, you have to straighten up. It is so tough out there that if an appointment cannot be moved or changed to accommodate you, then get to the appointment regardless of any excuse. If some of these excuses are legitimate and unfortunate, then by all means, reschedule your appointment. If you are legitimately feeling ill, it will reflect on your reading. Phone your agent immediately and if the role is not being cast that day, then re-schedule. Most casting directors are reasonable and will accommodate a problem. Everyone in life today with the exception of Opera Winfrey has a cell phone, so call the casting office direct if you are running late for a legitimate reason. Seasoned actors, such as Debbie Reynolds, can alter their shows due to sickness without fully canceling them. I worked with Debbie on a benefit for the City of Hope. Debbie was very ill with 104 temperature, the flu and laryngitis and I insisted that she cut her show down or not appear at all. She agreed to cut three numbers, but went on with the show nevertheless. On another occasion, Debbie and I were working on a road company production of "The Unsinkable Molly

Brown." Debbie went on stage with a high temperature and pneumonia. Fortunately, we closed for the Christmas holiday and Debbie recovered during that time off.

When Frank Sinatra's mother was killed in a private plane crash on her way to his show in Las Vegas—Mr. Sinatra was told about the tragedy.

He went on with the show and that's just part of being a professional.

Despite the image that some egotistical casting directors may give, we are mere mortals just like you. We have the same sets of problems as you, so there is no need to put the casting director on some kind of pedestal. Be yourself, and if they give you attitude—ride with it. You will meet some very professional and classy casting directors in the 21ˢᵗ century, and unfortunately you will also meet some ego-crazed fly by nights. Remember to keep your cool at all times and do not give attitude. One of the most frequent complaints (on a list of many) that I receive from actors about casting directors is that when the casting director is reading a scene or side with the actor, the c.d. never looks up at the actor. No eye contact. What do you do? Do not despair— some people are nice and some are not. For every one unfriendly casting director, you will meet 3 very actor friendly casting directors. There are many veterans still out there including the famous Lynn Stalmaster who is basically "retired," but can be "wooed" back to casting for a great script. In my opinion, I believe that Lynn always represented the very highest in taste, class, knowledge, sensitivity and actor friendliness. So naturally, this leads me into the next phase of some people's lives—"How do I become a casting director?" I have monthly phone calls from all over the country—college grads wanting to get into the casting profession. How? Read on.

Go to www.CastingSociety.com) and learn how you may "intern" and other suggestions on 'how to get into casting. And – read the next chapter.

CHAPTER NINETEEN

Any News????

After you are finished reading with a casting director and they say, "Well, we'll see what happens" or "Gee, nice reading, thank you for coming in," do not start bugging them!

"Do I have the job"? "When will I know"? "Was I that good"?

"Can I read it again"? "Should I read for another role"? STOP

Get over you!

Also, do yourself a favor and do not be a yenta. If you do not know what a yenta is, then let me explain. A yenta is a Yiddish word meaning "busybody" or "tattletale." or someone who "gossips". Why is it that five actors leave my office and if they were to be interviewed by a network newscaster in my parking lot, they would all tell the newscaster that they just booked the job? When I was starting out in the business, I let my entire circle of close friends know what was going on in my career. The mistake then, that I know now, is that I too was a yenta! AND, some of the people I thought were friends, were the back stabbers and the duplicitous people I should NOT have trusted as friends. Be judicious about what you share and with whom.

Keep your mouth shut until your agent phones you and says "Hello actor, you booked the job with Casting Director Joe."

First of all, don't take power out of the moment. Give that to yourself. It will give you confidence in your work. You earned the job, so enjoy it.

We have all been embarrassed at some time in our life when we thought that a job had been booked, and it falls through later on. In the meantime, you have called everyone you possibly know to tell them that you got a job. Wait until you get the job before you spread the news.

Mind your own business and let other actors mind theirs. If you know of a role that you are not right for, be generous and tell a friend about it. IF they are prepared to go in and possible book the job. It's good Karma and will come back to you. Let them phone their agent and inquire about the role—if they are right for it—perhaps they will get an audition. Project some classiness.

Keep your professional life to yourself and to those closest to you. Hang with the people, and network with those who support you the most, not suck you dry of your enthusiasm.

There is a distinct difference in being an actor who "shares" and an actor who is self-serving.

Here is a scenario: Your agent calls and says that there is a role in a feature film being cast playing the sibling to Robert Redford,

Paul Newman, or Brad Pitt. You are perfect for the third or fourth lead and you must get to 20th Century Fox immediately to meet the casting director.

You break your neck trying to find something to wear, cut yourself shaving (face or legs), trip over a chair and break your little toe in your mania, and are made aware that your car battery is dead. You decide to grab a cab and go to the audition.

You arrive at the audition and look at the script (or in some cases you have the opportunity of taking the script with you to study

73 "So You Wanna Be An Actor . . . Act Like One" for some allocated time period) and begin preparing for the big moment—he reading.

According to the Screen Actor's Guild contract, an actor is permitted to see a full script 24 hours prior to a reading or meeting. AND, if a script is not available to be taken out of a casting director's office—it is available at the office to read. So now you have calmed yourself down and you know that this is the role that was sent to you from God above. You walk in the door and your heart starts sending the blood pumping through your brain "This is it! This is it!" screams your brain. Houses, limos, clothes, money, what you want could be yours. Before you open up your mouth you are picturing yourself in a new Mercedes. You go in and give what you consider to be the most amazing reading of your life and you leave exhilarated. Days pass. Wine, drugs, sleepless nights, hundreds of phone calls to your friends telling them about the good news. Fantasy time.

Then the phone DOES finally ring. You are not rich and famous yet, which means that you have not hired your butler, and therefore must pick up the phone with your own two little hands. You pick it up and it's your agent. Sam Schmuck. Like a foghorn in your ear your agent says, "I just spoke with so and so and they thought that the reading was fabulous. Your look is sensational. While this chatter is going on you are thinking,

"Money, Europe, eekend." While you are NOT listening, the agent continues—"but you didn't get the job because you are Caucasian and the writer just decided to make this character African American. You were so overwhelmed with excitement that you just tuned out the rest of the conversation.

At this point in time, you hang up the phone and you start thinking about a) killing yourself; b) getting out of the business; c) phoning the casting director and begging profusely; or d) all of the above.

You honestly believe that your career is over and that you will never work again. Let us stop for a moment and take a look at this situation. First of all, get a grip. This is only one role that you did not book. There will be many more opportunities—IF you keep up with your profession. You have to get into your head that this is a business. Whether it is a budget problem, you have the wrong look; your acting was not on the mark, whatever it may be at that moment, not getting the part is not the end of the world. Remember, confidence and everything that goes with it is vitally important. Use it and do not get yourself down.

Don't be arrogant and cocky—that is not the message here. Be realistic. Let me share an inside story about the day I left my job at Columbia Pictures Television. In my head this was equivalent to just having lost my best friend. Having packed all of my things, I left my office and prepared to enter into the independent casting business with my partner Al Onorato. I went home, took a shower, fixed a bowl of popcorn, sat in my den staring into space and waited for a sign. No sign came, but the phone rang. It was my agent Amy Grossman from Creative Artists Agency. "What are you doing home at this time of the day?" She asked? "I am sitting in my bathrobe, eating popcorn, staring into space and waiting for you to call me, if you must know," I replied. My career is over.

Well, Amy set me straight immediately by teaching me an important lesson. The credibility that my partner Al and I had earned through the years would be rewarded by support from the industry. Amy was correct.

The following day when the trade papers carried the announcement that Al and I had departed Columbia Pictures Television (front page I might add!!!) our respective phones at home did not stop ringing. By day's end, we had several job offers, including one from 20th Century Fox where we signed a long term contract and our careers became even more successful than ever.

CHAPTER TWENTY

The Actress Hated The Script And Lost The Job

——————

I feel certain that some of you think I must be a lunatic with a chapter heading such as this one. Well, perhaps if you read this chapter and think about it, you might save yourself from looking like the missing village idiot!

There was a wonderful man named Larry Tucker. Larry was an awardwinning writer. One of his most successful screenplays that rates as one of AFI's (American Film Institute) favorite 100, "Ted and Alice"

I was very happy to be working with Larry and his partner Larry Rosen on a pilot, which Tucker had written and Rosen was producing.

So, I began the interview session and politely, as we did in those days, introduced both Larry and Larry to this actress who was known as a commodity to the networks. She had a couple of failed series and was no winner of an actress but had a huge likeability quotient. (Formerly known as TVQ)

This actress,—let's call her Joan, as in mean old Joan Crawford, had no idea who anyone in the room was, either by name or title. I did introduce the third gentleman as the director.

I asked this actress Joan if she had any questions regarding her character.

"No" she said—"Let's just read"

Fine, so I proceeded to give her a line and she responded and we were about one minute into the dialogue, when old Joan THREW the sides at me and said in a most agitated voice "I can't read this shit!"

If the floor had opened up, I would have gladly fallen through.

But worst was to follow.

As the writer, producer and director all looked at me with this "Now what do we do Jerry?" look, my assistant rang through that news had arrived that my father had just passed away. That was my out!

I said, "Thank you very much Joan; thank you for coming in."

She was outta there. I left the office and obviously old Joan was never to be heard of again in my office at least.

The other famous dumb actor story I tell is when I invited one of my favorite young character actors into a reading for a Movie of the Week at Columbia Pictures Television. A terrific script, a solid cast being put together and a drop dead roll for this guy who was on the money â•" both in look, edge, attitude and acting chops.

I asked my usual courtesy question: "Have you any questions for me or for our director? 'No, thank you Jerry,' he responded.

At this point the director said I wonder if you might really play this character with more edge than indicated in the script?

I would prefer to do it the way I saw it originally with my own take on the character said this actor.

My face flushed and I asked that we proceed ahead. The reading was quite special and it was obvious to everyone in the room that we had found the right actor.

The Director dismissed the actor so quickly that my red face and head actually spun around. No thank you, just silence.

The actor insulted the Director and it took me three weeks to turn his head around along with a phone call apology from the actor to the director.

What is the point of these stories? Don't be a jerk. Unless you are a psychic or know everyone in the world, you may not know for whom you are reading. Don't EVER criticize any material in front of people you don't know, and for God's sake, not in a reading. Additionally, if a producer, director or casting director is gracious enough to give you an adjustment" (note) take the suggestion and deal with it. Take it as a compliment that whomever gives you the note sees something about you that they like. Perhaps you have the right look, right height right whatever—don't sabotage yourself and lose the opportunity or even the job.

A question about the script, yes, a request to change a word, yes, tell a roomful of people that you "Can't read this shit." NO! Tell a director, you're read it your own way—NO!

Actor's forget that casting directors are on THEIR side leave your egos at the door and read the script the way it is written— you are not the writer—use some simple "manners".

Through almost 30 years, I have witnessed sensational readings:

Book this actor: send him to wardrobe, I'm thinking. The actor leaves the room and the director or producer says, "I never ever want to see that actor again as long as I live." Directors have egos too, you'll find out as you go through your careers and have what is commonly termed as "creative differences." The director wants you to take his suggestion and you have your own choices.

"Think before you speak . . . . think before you speak

CHAPTER TWENTY-ONE

To Cut Or Not To Cut . . . Cosmetic Surgery

- - - - -

I recall an actor friend approaching me in the late 70's asking whether or not I thought he should get a nose job? I asked why he would consider a nose job? He had a pretty hooked honker and considered the idea that perhaps changing his appearance would expand his chances of playing roles other than the 'character' ones he was booking. My thought at the time was—

"'Why bother?'—My opinion has since changed. When I was 18 years old and saved enough money, I rushed to a cosmetic surgeon to discuss having my ears pinned back. Growing up, I was called "Dumbo" because I had protruding ears and not until I was in high school did I understand the psychological effect the teasing had on me. I also recall vividly after having my ears pinned back, the feeling of being much more secure in my looks and with that feeling, I also gained a great deal of confidence in myself. Now in the 21st century, a recent statistic revealed that just as many men if not more—than women are having cosmetic surgery. Do I think it is necessary? I do not sit in judgment— and quite frankly, it matters not what anyone else thinks. If YOU feel that something could use improvement, then by all means—go for it.

Men have been spending money for many years on hairpieces— and women as well are spending millions of dollars a year to improve their looks as well as their image. As liberal a person as I am—I do feel that women over 60 should NOT wear strapless gowns—and men over 50 should NOT wear a Speedo. On the other side of the coin—I try not to sit in judgment of anyone. I call these examples poor taste. Not everyone can be a gorgeous leading lady or a handsome leading man and on the other hand—if we all looked alike—casting actors would be a lottery system. Be happy with what you have—IF—you are psychologically 'stuck' with some physical issue—then see your physician and discuss the issue. I am talking about weight issues here—if you are anorexic or bulimic—go and get help NOW— this is a psychological and serious medical problem. I love Camaryn Manheim as an actress, and quite frankly, not until she accepted an Emmy and stated "This is for the big ladies"—did I ever think of her as a "large lady". I thought of her as a wonderful actress. Be cautious about your choices of cosmetic surgery—not unlike Marlene Dietrich who stated "I vant to be alone"—many people look in the mirror one day and decide that they don't wish anyone to see them again—and they become reclusive. For myself—I'm very happy with my looks at this point in my life—I obsessed for too many years about my receding hairline and now Look at two of my favorite actors—Kevin Spacey and Bruce Willis who have made receding hairlines and baldheads sexy for men.

Get opinions; discuss with your physicians and cosmetic surgeons and then go with your gut instinct. Scars, wrinkles, bald heads, moles, pocked skin can all be assets to an actors—think about it—and get professional opinions before you start "cutting".

A long time actor friend of mine entered my office in 1978 to ask my opinion about his nose.

"What about your nose?" I inquired.

"Jer, do you think a nose job would help my chances of doing "leading man' roles?"

Well, my friend did have quite a honker, so let me give you some background.

My pal Peter was a successful young character actor working like crazy. A funny guy, a solid actor, he did commerical and sitcoms and the "character" type roles available.

81 "So You Wanna Be An Actor . . . Act Like One"

"Why would you even consider changing your nose? What would happen if you get a botched up job?" I asked.

"I really want to go out for leading man roles, and as long as my comedy holds, why not be a better looking character actor as well as a leading man?"

Well, Peter went ahead and had his nose job—very good cosmetic work; changed his entire look and he became a very handsome leading man. Today he is a very successful producer and writer.

In those days I suspect that casting directors, including myself, were caught up in the Barbie and Ken doll plastic perfect look.

In today's world of casting, anything goes (non-traditional casting). Steve Martin is not exactly a character actor. He is a good-looking guy who can play both drama and comedy.

Do I know the answer to your question of whether or not to have a cosmetic surgical procedure done? No I don't, BUT—I do have some advice.

Get at least two opinions from reputable, referred to you by family or friend's cosmetic surgeon.

For me—when I had been teased my entire childhood about my "dumbo ears", I had them pinned back. Did it change me? Yes, it did. My confidence level was higher and I didn't feel unattractive. If a cosmetic procedure will enhance not only your looks, but your inner confidence—go for it.

Should you consider cosmetic surgery?

Self-esteem is one of the elements, which makes up the foundation of one's ego. (Here is the shrink speaking)—My opinion has always been "do as you wish—only if it will make YOU fell better". Be cautious not to get into the every 6-month "nip and tuck" syndrome—dangerous—see a shrink first.

Let's also hit on 'competition' for a moment.

There is no competition. Why? Because no one looks exactly like you—and you look like you—not them—get it?! So competition is a very subjective word. Casting is a very subjective profession— and as I mentioned in an earlier chapter—no one ever knows why they didn't book a job—assuming all candidates were equal in their acting skills. Remember the story of the actress whom the director felt had "one lazy eye?"—I rest my case.

In closing out this chapter, my sense is—if you are 'obsessed' with having some work done, then do it. Do it for yourself and don't bother with what anyone else thinks.

Be advised that any change physically will alter you internally.

Any ethical cosmetic surgeon will cross examine you as to reasons why you feel you need work done.

We are in the 21st century when now, more than ever, men are having just as much work done as women.

By the way, should you decide to have surgery performed—less is more and the best compliment you could be given "post" surgery is "how rested you look"—(face lift). Cosmetic surgery should enhance gently, not radically.

One more consideration in changing one's looks as one ages. Do you as an actor wish to grow older naturally and broaden your roles? If you have played 35 year old for many years and you are now 50, do you wish to go into different roles or try for those 35 year old one? In my opinion, there are enough actors legitimately 35 years old.

Academy Award winner, Shelley Winters, one of the beauties of her time and a great actress, just "let herself be herself ". it didn't hurt her career—same goes for Gregory Peck, Paul Newman and so many others.

Again—think before you "cut"!! and good luck!

CHAPTER TWENTY-TWO

Getting Personal With Jerry*

Some personal answers from Jerry *these questions were asked of me by Eric Vollweiler, a college student at Emerson College in Boston, Massachusetts—and about 100 other people throughout my career!

Favorite all time actors: Spencer Tracey/Tom Hanks

Favorite all time actress: Meryl Streep, Bette Davis

Classiest actor Cary Grant, Raphael Spbarge, George Clooney, Hugh

Classiest actress—Audrey Hepburn, Leslie Hope

Favorite films: Forrest Gump, The Shawshank Redemption, The Godfather 1, Casablanca, Citizen Kane, Pretty Woman" and "Driving Miss Daisy" – amongst other's on the top of the list.

Who is your role model? That would be my friend Ronald as well as General Colin Powell. q) Had you become an actor, whom would you have emulated? a) Tim Robbins with Alec Baldwin's head on Tim's body.

Favorite Network Executive: Brandon Tartikoff (1949-1997), Former President NBC Entertainment

Most influence on your career—Mike Donohew, Al Onorato, Ron Meyer, Renee

Valente, Ruta Lee, Debbie Reynolds, John Bowab and the late Jack Haley, Jr.

Best ensemble casting: The Today Show *my editor argued this answer with me. Why do I consider The Today Show the best ensemble casting? My answer is that typically the best ensembles of which there have been and are many hold an audience's interest for a 1/2 hour or one hour. The Today Show holds audience's attention for 15 hours per week.

Questions and Answers from 25 years of teaching and public speaking: Q) Why did you become a casting director? Because secretly, I always wanted to be a song and dance man. BUT—I didn't have the talent. I have always looked up to and admired actors because of their skills and risk-taking. I have always loved working with actors to this date. Also, because of my love of the human emotions—and the respect for people who can open their mouths and make a writer's line and character come to life—an extraordinary gift. Q) What do you like most about your job and what don't you like about your job? I love meeting new talent and watching them grows. What I don't like is the "judgment calls" that must go along with my profession. Q) Out of all of your projects thus far, are there any moments, events that are "Hallmark" moments? The opportunity to work with Lucille Ball, Bob Hope, Robert Mitchum, Lana Turner, Fred MacMurray, Robert Preston, Ann-Margret, Lisa Minelli, and thousands of other actors, Marvin Hamlisch, Presidents Ford and Reagan, Julian Bond, and the Hallmark of all—Colin Powell have made me realize how lucky I am in my chosen profession.

Q) What is the singles best piece of advice that you can give to an actor? Always be honest, keep your integrity and think before you speak.

Q) If an actor has not had a chance to look over the sides for whatever reason, should he ask for extra time, and if so, how much?

With all of the state of the art ways to obtain sides (on line, facsimile, in person) there is little excuse for not receiving sides.

However, there are exceptions. In this particular case, I think two hours is enough time for an actor to study and make choices on material.

Q) Do you frown on an actor who tries to change his appointment time for a personal reason? Absolutely not. If an actor has a legitimate reason for wishing to change an appointment time "fine—just don't abuse the privilege.

Q) What's the best thing to do after giving your reading? Is there anything or should I just say thank you & leave? Thank the people in the office and leave if they want you to read material again they will ask. NEVER EVER ask to read for another role. (See chapter ay Goodnight Gracie) Q) What's the best way to get a GOOD agent? In this day and age, the best shot at getting a good agent is to have tape or a DVD or VCR on yourself. One might luck out and have an agent see them in a play or workshop or college production. Q) How does an actor find his/her most marketable qualities and then utilize them to their fullest? I think that we all know what our most marketable qualities are. My teeth, smile and sense of humor have done wonders for me. I look at the eyes first—choose your best quality and soar with it. Perhaps you have an engaging personality, perhaps you have special eyes, voice, style of dress—only you know what shines best about yourself.

Q) When preparing for an interview, how should I dress? Dress in the manner in which you would go to any professional meeting. That does not mean high heels or suit and tie, breasts exposed or inappropriate attire, like a bathing suit, shorts, etc.

Q) Say you're doing a speech in an office for someone and it's not necessarily directed toward an audience, is an advantage/ disadvantage to cheat your eye toward the auditor? I believe you are talking about a onologue I personally do not like to be the focal point of a monologue I prefer studying the actor. The best practice I have found is to ask. If the person to whom you are reading does not wish to be the focal point, then find one—a pencil on the desk—a piece of furniture, or perhaps a hanging on the wall.

Q) On perhaps the second or third callback when you're really familiar with the material (sides) should you just hold it or once or twice look down at it or look at it only if you forget your place. Never ever read without holding a side in your hand.

Actors are not required to memorize material before they get on the set. It doesn't matter whether or not you know the material with your eyes closed always hold your sides (material).

Q) If you've read a piece one way for the auditioners and they are willing to have you do it again in another manner, how far is it prudent to go with it? A few twists or something out on another limb? Use your brains and listen. When the auditioner suggests another way to read the scene, LISTEN and be clear.

Ask if you do not understand what they are looking for. Always remember that less is more. Don't overact, don't get stagy, and use your own instinct. Q) When reading with a casting director, is it ever advisable to suggest a change in the way he or she is reading to you if you see in that will help your reading? Casting directors are not actors. One of the most frequent complaints actors have is that the reader is looking down at the material and not at the actor. NEVER suggest to anyone reading with you how they should read do the best you can and do not let the reader's lack of acting ability deter you from doing good work.

Q) Why do casting directors have all these horror stories of actors who commit cardinal sins at auditions? Obviously, these actors are being called in. WHY are they being called in? I've never committed a single faux pas in the entire 37 years I've been acting, and I get called in roughly as often as elections are held. What gives? This is one of the downfalls of acting. In the 21st century aside from the reality shows, most demographics ask for and younger faces, this is not to say that there is not enough work for a more mature actor there is it is just that the competition gets heavier as one ages.

Q) Is there an unspoken actors caste system? With rare exception, actors who are on top seem to have always been on top, no matter how mediocre they or their films might get. 99% of actors who take smaller roles in films seem never to be heard from again. Who's behind this? Martians? The brotherhood of masons with their secret handshakes? What's going on here? If there is an unspoken caste system, someone might tell me about it. I think not. The actors on top all started on the bottom do your research Matt Damon and Ben Affleck didn't just appear and win an Oscar. They had study and work behind them.

Q) What qualities do you look for in actor's performance, personality and character? One thing—believability.

Q) If you were an actor in Hollywood, how would you pursue your career? What means would you use? If I were an actor in Hollywood, I would study hard enough until I was ready to go on auditions and then do theatre and hope to be seen by an agent, casting director or producer. Someone will see someone in a theatre production and the career will take off.

Q) Can you detect a future as well as exceptional actors (or rather who will be the exceptional ones)? I'm no psychic, but any casting director who has instinct will immediately recognize an actor's ability.

Q) What is the best way for a starting actor to conduct himself on the set? Keep quiet and keep still, listen and watch and stay out of the way until you are called for your scene. It's called learning.

Q) What is the single most important thing an actor should know and be prepared for in an audition? An actor should only come in with honesty with himself and as the character.

Q) Do you like "ICS" (Interesting choices that aren't necessarily) indicated in the script? This is a new one on me. I've never heard the expression. Ask the casting director or director if you might stretch the character—if they say, fine go with it otherwise, use your head and make the appropriate choices.

Q) Do you have any particular technique that you know works for actors to calm oneself—or focus before an audition? Actors have different ways of calming themselves down. I don't think there is one stock answer. For me, when I need to deliver a speech and sense some stage fright I typically turn the fear into concentration and focus on what I am going to be discussing in front of the audience.

Q) Would you prefer people to get physical or to demonstrate behavior or rather to sit and simply connect? Less is more: just be the character or just be yourself. If material indicates physicality, NEVER ever touch a reader (casting director, director, etc). Just be in the moment and don't become overly dramatic.

Q) What tips can you offer to an aspiring actor when one has an 8-hour day-job?

Good question. I would be upfront with your boss and advise that there may be days that you will have to leave for appointments.

Perhaps you could rade your lunch hour at noon for a reading or meeting at 3pm. Don't lie—tell the truth most bosses who hire actors are used to the appointments during the day.

Q) When dealing with agents, what qualities do you prefer they have, whom do you like to deal with? All I ask for is honesty. I have relied on agents through my entire career to guide me to the right actors. If an agent burns me by sending an actor I've not met into my office and the actor should not be out on auditions, I let the agent get by once—hurt me once, shame on you—hurt me twice, shame on me.

Q) How often should we keep in touch with postcards? I personally like the postcard system. It is recommended strongly that actors NOT phone a casting office. Drop in's are also frowned upon. A postcard when you are appearing on TV or in a stage production or have changed representation or contact information is the perfect opportunity for a mailing. Q) Would you consider hiring an actor that doesn't have representation (an agent?) Granted that you saw their work and liked it? I've always had an open door policy. If I see a photo I like or a resume I find interesting; it doesn't matter to me. Better yet; if I see an actor in a stage production or in another vehicle, of course it doesn't matter whether or not he/she has any representation.

Q) Do you and other casting directors hold grudges against actors because of their relationships with an agent you don't like?

I can only speak for myself. I hold no grudges ever. I've had one or two occasions over the years that I've asked an actor to leave my office and these were the most isolated incidences when they crashed" auditions!—A Big fat no no!

Q) Do you frown upon extra work? And if so, why? Not only do I not frown upon extra work, I think its' a good learning tool.
Up and coming actors have to make a living the money is good, but more than that, you get to see how projects come to fruition and get to watch other actors work more learning. I totally support extra work

Q) If you are not SAG how is the best way to get a theatrical agent? It doesn't matter whether you are SAG or not. The 21st century is the toughest time I remember in getting representation. Having tape is a solid bet, and even that sometimes doesn't get one an agent.

Q) If you do not have a theatrical agent, how is the (I'm sure he means to say, "what is" but nevertheless) best way to get auditions with casting directors? I commented in the chapter on gents that this is the most frequently asked question. There is no way to outguess who will or will not be in an audience. I still say, do theatre and daytime drama then send out mass mailings or postcards and do mass mailings of headshots and resumes, two or three times a year statistically, someone will call you in for an appointment. no? Say you? That doesn't work? Pray hard!

Q) Do you think the "2-for photo (2 smaller headshots on the 8x10) is a good preferable to 2-8x10 different headshots? I'm amazed at the expression. The 8 x 10, plain old black and white is fine—see the chapter on photos Q) Do you like to cast "against type" when the actor does a great job to convince you to? Duh—yes. I've always supported from the earliest days nontraditional casting. There is no reason that a woman cannot be anything a man can be except a father and vice versa

Q) Do you prefer casting actors with more TV and Film credits than without? Of course, we all want to hire actors with experience, BUT, this does not mean that I who support the theatre actor will not cast theatre actors

Q) Do you like to use actors that you like more than once? I've re-hired actors over the years if they are right for a role, they get called in, whether I've worked with them once or 10 times

Q) As a casting director please give advice on how an actor can upgrade their status. Meaning if an actor were considered in the under-five category and/or afternoon drama category only, how would we impress and or convince those powers that be that we can do mainstream? A casting director can look at tape of something an under actor has done. Every actor I know started out with a one liner including Harrison Ford and David Hasselhoff

Q) Do producers (to the best of your knowledge) make judgments on actors brought in on their resume Representation?

Meaning, does a producer assume an actor is better, not just by the actors audition, but by who is his representation and who hired him before? I think it is obvious that if an actor is represented by a high-powered large agency, the agent sees something in them. However, that does not play in my office.

Many casting directors bring in actors from the smallest agencies in the city. Have a good photo and honest resume; the name or status of the agent will not interfere in most casting offices.

Q) There is an "A" list of actors, which means there must be a "B" list. Is there a "C" "D" and "E" list? How do you start? How do you move up? In all honesty, patience, time and luck, providing you can act. Q) What would you think makes a good actor other than the obvious? (A special trait) Tough question.

See the chapter on A Gift From God

Q) How open-minded are you about seeing actors as entirely different characters? (Do you have a tendency to type cast)? (Honestly) See above answer re non-traditional casting). And that's honest!

Q) Is there any way that is not bothersome to the average casting director to get feedback after an audition? No—it is awkward for a c.d. to give feedback. A cordial thank you is nice—if a c.d. is overwhelmed by your performance, you will be acknowledged verbally or by a callback

Q) Since I have been in the biz for only 3 years, and my age range is early to mid-thirties, people assume my resume represents 10 or 12 years in the business—so it seems relatively weak. When they take the time to find out my resume represents only 3 years, then they've impressed. How should I handle this? I sense that you are telling me that people are impressed with your ability even though you have only been acting for three years. Take the compliments and don't worry about what is on your resume

Q) Are there any extra tips or things I can do to get more auditions for feature films and MOW's? It's all in a look—that's as honest as I can be. Film actors have film faces TV actors have TV faces what's the difference you ask? The difference is that a film face jumps off the screen or one cannot take their eyes off of some one.

Q) If you are with a good agent and have a chance to move up to a bigger agent, when do you know its' best to move up? This is one of the best questions of the day. I am a strong believer in loyalty. I think I will give you the answer that Cuba Gooding, Jr. said when receiving his Oscar. He thanked his first agent, Lorilee, Jr., for her support and also for guiding him to the right agent when his career started taking off. Agents are typically interested in money and how much you can make for them. If you like your agent and trust your agent, stay with your agent.
When an actor is hot, casting directors will find you whether you are with William Morris Agency or Minnie Mouse Agency.

Q) How important is videotape? In this day and age, it is vital.
Be advised that DVD's are now taking the place of inch just as inch took the place of inch videotape. Typically, agents will ask for tape before

working with an actor and videotape is an invaluable tool for casting directors in making decisions.

Q) Does it do any good to mail a picture and resume to a casting director for a show you think you are right for? I can only speak for myself. Unsolicited mailings have always been welcomed in my offices you have nothing to lose. I personally open every single envelope other casting directors may just work with agents but the only thing you can lose is a photo and resume in a wastebasket

Q) How can I get more readings for feature films? Submit a photo and resume that honestly represents you patience, time and luck again prevaile

Q) What can I do to get my agent more excited about me? Keep booking jobs

Q) Do you handle submissions directly and how do you process them? All envelopes with submissions whether by agents, personal managers or unsolicited are opened and reviewed. They are stacked into categories, usually who looks right for a role and those stacks of photos are reviewed and culled down sometimes more than a dozen times before I select my typically 5 choices per role.

Q) Do personalities keep you from hiring someone? I believe I answered this question earlier; I have had two isolated incidences of personality clashes

Q) What key points should an actor remember before entering an audition? See cheat sheet and just be yourself in the character's body.

CHAPTER TWENTY-THREE

No Limitations Please

‒ ‒ ‒ ‒ ‒ ‒

Actors have far too many "excuses" in my opinion. If it's not one thing, it's another—so I wanted to discuss "limitations" with you. Soar With Your Strengths, a book by my pal Paula Nelson is a great title which applies to all of us. If you are going to try to succeed as an actor OR in any other profession, please don't go in with "limitations" placed on yourself.

I went to a fundraising event last week which reminded me to add these few pages on a very sensitive topic. That being— medical or emotional "issues" or problems which might stand in an actor's way.

I use the word issues because some people deal with disorders in one way or another. I have worked with actors are visually or hearing impaired, HIV positive, full blown AIDS—and those dealing with cancer or diabetes.

The event last week was to raise funds for Turrets syndrome—a very distressing disorder caused by lack of "synapses" in the brain. It makes one inappropriately scream obsenities or "gibberish"—and/or leaves the person with jerking movements of the arms—blinking eyes and all sorts of physical "quirks".

Turrets syndrome falls into the category of OCD conditions— Obsessive, compulsive disorders.

Other areas which actor's must deal are—Down syndrome, dyslexia, ADD (Adult deficit disorder) stuttering, lisp, panic attacks, stage fright, fear of flying—any "limitation" which might alter their career or life style to a degree which is totally non-productive

I have worked with actors suffering from and/or dealing with all of the above. Thankfully, now in the 21st century, the pharmaceutical world of wonders helps countless millions of people all over the world with all of the aforementioned problems.

When I was 12 years old, I went on a school trip to New York City, a two hour trip from the Jersey shore—where Danny DeVito, Jack Nicholson, Bruce Springsteen and I spent our 'growing up' years.

Upon my return to the school ground where my Dad waited for my twin sister and me to depart from our respective buses, I stepped into a world of 42 years of hell. Panic attack, ODC, agoraphobia. Life altering "issues" due to what we now know is chemical deficiencies in the brain and are easily treatable.

Kim Basinger with whom I worked on "From here To Eternity" TV series—and the very talented, bright and gifted Donny Osmond, my pal Florence Henderson (Mrs. Brady) a couple of very successful politicians I am acquainted with—and the list goes on. All of us have gone through the same kind of hell. Was it limiting to us? Yes—very—and here we all are to talk about it.

The point is—get help with whatever "issues" you have. There is help out there for everyone—new meds for migraines, PMS, alcoholism, drug addiction and the big mama of all "depression".

I often wonder if some of the actors from the 1920's to the 1980's suffering from alcoholism and drug addiction, complexes we have never heard of—all due to chemical imbalances would have been better actors? I sense so.

In the old days, those of us suffering from chemical imbalances were thrown into the category of schizophrenia—today, everything is lumped into bi-polar disorders. Why even bother to discuss this topic? Because for those of you hiding in the 97 "So You Wanna Be An Actor . . . Act Like One" closet or suffering from whatever—bulimia and other eating disorders, depression, post partum or generalized—get help—it is readily available.

Don't ever be afraid to let the casting director or assistant director on the set know that you have "special needs" like— insulin intake, drops for your eyes if you happen to have glaucoma—you get my message.

Stop hiding behind your dyslexia—get your sides early and see you Doctor. Tom Cruise is a big time dyslexic actor and has dealt with it.

Michael J. Fox suffers from Parkinson's disease and continues to make appearance—despite his "limitation".

If you are not well and have an interview—tell your agent— change the appointment. A sensitive casting director will clearly understand. If you are working and ill—tough titty—the show must go on. Too many famous stories to relate about the Gene Kelly's of the world whose dance in the rain with 102-degree temperature—didn't stop production—and the film is today considered the number one musical of all time. (See Imdb. com—Singing' In The Rain).

You are NOT going to kill your chances of booking a role if you have to take a break for an insulin shot.

Having sat on the California governor's Committee on Disabilities, it was with the late Ethel Winant, Paul Waginer and others that we pushed through legislation and awareness in the industry—why couldn't a wheelchair bound actor sit behind a desk and play any given number of roles? Why couldn't a hearing impaired actor work?

My buddy Carrie Fisher "came out of the closet" with her chemical imbalances—and now under control—she leads a very happy and productive life.

Is there help for any actor with any type of "limitation"?

Obviously, just don't stand in your own way.

No excuses.

When my own chemical imbalances were replaced by a magic bullet medication my physician discovered in 1999, my entire life changed. When sharing the news of this remarkable find with a confidante, I said "I have no idea how I got through school" and she replied "school"—how the hell did you get through life?"

NO LIMITATIONS PERMITTED—you are in a profession with no boundaries—just don't ever limit yourselves!! jf

June 004

There is no one out there exactly like you or me. I am rewriting this particular page in memory of an extraordinary boy of 13 years old named Mattie Stepanek who died this past week. I am writing this page because Mattie verbalized audibly, the original title of this particular chapter "Each of us is unique as we are".

Mattie had his wishes granted and in my own personal belief system, I'm sure he is looking down from Heaven overlooking others in achieving their own dreams become realities. As you strive and achieve, learn to give back—it's a wonderful feeling.

Here is a boy who "got it"—got what life is all about and he just continues to inspire me—even at my age. Take a lesson from Mattie—go for your own personal "Heart Songs". Jf

April 22, 2004

In honor and memory of my family friend Pat Tillman whose vision was to:

"Inspire and support others striving to promote positive change in themselves and the world around them." (www.PatTillmanfoundation.com)

January, 2005

May 20, 2005

READ YOUR SIDES IN THE WAITING ROOM AND STOP "COMPARING" IF EVERYONE WERE NOT DIFFERENT IN SOME WAY-CASTING WOULD BE A LOTTERY

MRS. REAGAN/MRS. FORD/ THE WORD CANCER AND IN PARTICULAR BREAST CANCER WAS NOT DISCUSSED IN THE 80'S-NOT UNLIKE AIDS IN THE BEGINNING-SOME OF YOU READING THIS BOOK HAVE NO IDEA OF HOW PRIMITIVE WE ARE ABOUT CERTAIN SUBJECTS-AUTISM HAS JUST COME OUT OF THE CLOSET-AND BELIEVE IT OR NOT-I PUT TWO OF MY STUDENTS IN A PRODUCTION OF 'GREASE' AND THEY DID JUST FINE!!

THERE ARE PAST AND PRESENT ACTORS WHO "HIDE" ILLNESS FOR FEAR THAT THEY WON'T WORK ONCE THE WORD GETS OUT-ODDLY ENOUGH-TIMES HAVE CHANGED-MICHAEL J. FOX HAS A NEW SERIES ON THE AIR-WE HIRED A WONDERFUL ACTRESS NAMED MADELYN RHUE FOR MANY EPISODES OF 'FAME' AND WORKED AROUND HER DISABILITY-SHE WAS SUFFERING FROM M.S.-WE HIRED A BLIND ACTRESS IN A COURTROOM SCENE-AND NO ONE EVER KNEW THAT SHE HAD NO SIGHT-

THE MEDIA ACCESS OFFICE COMES TO BEING!

Recommendations

I highly recommend a book entitled "When God Winks"-by SQire Fridell, former President of ABC Network when I was entering the biz i winning writer. One of his most successful screenplays that rates as one of AFI's (American Film Institute) favorite 100, "Ted and Alice"

I was very happy to be working with Larry and his partner Larry Rosen on a pilot, which Tucker had written and Rosen was producing.

So, I began the interview session and politely, as we did in those days, introduced both Larry and Larry to this actress who was known as a commodity to the networks. She had a couple of failed series and was no winner of an actress but had a huge likeability quotient. (Formerly known as TVQ)

This actress,—let's call her Joan, as in mean old Joan Crawford, had no idea who anyone in the room was, either by name or title. I did introduce the third gentleman as the director.

I asked this actress Joan if she had any questions regarding her character.

76 JEROLD FRANKS

"No" she said—"Let's just read"

Fine, so I proceeded to give her a line and she responded and we were about one minute into the dialogue, when old Joan THREW the sides at me and said in a most agitated voice "I can't read this shit!"

If the floor had opened up, I would have gladly fallen through.

But worst was to follow.

As the writer, producer and director all looked at me with this "Now what do we do Jerry?" look, my assistant rang through that news had arrived that my father had just passed away. That was my out!

I said, "Thank you very much Joan; thank you for coming in."

She was outta there. I left the office and obviously old Joan was never to be heard of again in my office at least.

The other famous dumb actor story I tell is when I invited one of my favorite young character actors into a reading for a Movie of the Week at Columbia Pictures Television. A terrific script, a solid cast being put together and a drop dead roll for this guy who was on the money â•" both in look, edge, attitude and acting chops.

I asked my usual courtesy question: "Have you any questions for me or for our director? 'No, thank you Jerry,' he responded.

At this point the director said I wonder if you might really play this character with more edge than indicated in the script?

I would prefer to do it the way I saw it originally with my own take on the character said this actor.

My face flushed and I asked that we proceed ahead. The reading was quite special and it was obvious to everyone in the room that we had found the right actor.

The Director dismissed the actor so quickly that my red face and head actually spun around. No thank you, just silence.

The actor insulted the Director and it took me three weeks to turn his head around along with a phone call apology from the actor to the director.

What is the point of these stories? Don't be a jerk. Unless you are a psychic or know everyone in the world, you may not know for whom you are reading. Don't EVER criticize any material in front of people you don't know, and for God's sake, not in a reading. Additionally, if a producer, director or casting director is gracious enough to give you an adjustment" (note) take the suggestion and deal with it. Take it as a compliment that whomever gives you the note sees something about you that they like. Perhaps you have the right look, right height right whatever—don't sabotage yourself and lose the opportunity or even the job.

A question about the script, yes, a request to change a word, yes, tell a roomful of people that you "Can't read this shit." NO! Tell a director, you're read it your own way—NO!

Actor's forget that casting directors are on THEIR side leave your egos at the door and read the script the way it is written— you are not the writer—use some simple "manners".

Through almost 30 years, I have witnessed sensational readings:

Book this actor: send him to wardrobe, I'm thinking. The actor leaves the room and the director or producer says, "I never ever want to see that actor again as long as I live." Directors have egos too, you'll find out as you go through your careers and have what is commonly termed as "creative differences." The director wants you to take his suggestion and you have your own choices.

"Think before you speak . . . . think before you speak . . . ."

CHAPTER TWENTY-FOUR

To Cut Or Not To Cut . . . Cosmetic Surgery

I recall an actor friend approaching me in the late 70's asking whether or not I thought he should get a nose job? I asked why he would consider a nose job? He had a pretty hooked honker and considered the idea that perhaps changing his appearance would expand his chances of playing roles other than the 'character' ones he was booking. My thought at the time was—

"'Why bother?"—My opinion has since changed. When I was 18 years old and saved enough money, I rushed to a cosmetic surgeon to discuss having my ears pinned back. Growing up, I was called "Dumbo" because I had protruding ears and not until I was in high school did I understand the psychological effect the teasing had on me. I also recall vividly after having my ears pinned back, the feeling of being much more secure in my looks and with that feeling, I also gained a great deal of confidence in myself. Now in the 21st century, a recent statistic revealed that just as many men if not more—than women are having cosmetic surgery. Do I think it is necessary? I do not sit in judgment— and quite frankly, it matters not what anyone else thinks. If YOU feel that something could use improvement, then by all means—go for it.

Men have been spending money for many years on hairpieces— and women as well are spending millions of dollars a year to improve their looks as well as their image. As liberal a person as I am—I do feel that women over 60 should NOT wear strapless gowns—and men over 50 should NOT wear a Speedo. On the other side of the coin—I try not to sit in judgment of anyone. I call these examples poor taste. Not everyone can be a gorgeous leading lady or a handsome leading man and on the other hand—if we all looked alike—casting actors would be a lottery system. Be happy with what you have—IF—you are psychologically 'stuck' with some physical issue—then see your physician and discuss the issue. I am talking about weight issues here—if you are anorexic or bulimic—go and get help NOW— this is a psychological and serious medical problem. I love Camaryn Manheim as an actress, and quite frankly, not until she accepted an Emmy and stated "This is for the big ladies"—did I ever think of her as a "large lady". I thought of her as a wonderful actress. Be cautious about your choices of cosmetic surgery—not unlike Marlene Dietrich who stated "I vant to be alone"—many people look in the mirror one day and decide that they don't wish anyone to see them again—and they become reclusive. For myself—I'm very happy with my looks at this point in my life—I obsessed for too many years about my receding hairline and now Look at two of my favorite actors—Kevin Spacey and Bruce Willis who have made receding hairlines and baldheads sexy for men.

Get opinions; discuss with your physicians and cosmetic surgeons and then go with your gut instinct. Scars, wrinkles, bald heads, moles, pocked skin can all be assets to an actors—think about it—and get professional opinions before you start "cutting".

A long time actor friend of mine entered my office in 1978 to ask my opinion about his nose.

"What about your nose?" I inquired.

"Jer, do you think a nose job would help my chances of doing "leading man' roles?"

Well, my friend did have quite a honker, so let me give you some background.

My pal Peter was a successful young character actor working like crazy. A funny guy, a solid actor, he did commerical and sitcoms and the "character" type roles available.

"Why would you even consider changing your nose? What would happen if you get a botched up job?" I asked.

"I really want to go out for leading man roles, and as long as my comedy holds, why not be a better looking character actor as well as a leading man?"

Well, Peter went ahead and had his nose job—very good cosmetic work; changed his entire look and he became a very handsome leading man. Today he is a very successful producer and writer.

In those days I suspect that casting directors, including myself, were caught up in the Barbie and Ken doll plastic perfect look.

In today's world of casting, anything goes (non-traditional casting). Steve Martin is not exactly a character actor. He is a good-looking guy who can play both drama and comedy.

Do I know the answer to your question of whether or not to have a cosmetic surgical procedure done? No I don't, BUT—I do have some advice.

Get at least two opinions from reputable, referred to you by family or friend's cosmetic surgeon.

For me—when I had been teased my entire childhood about my "dumbo ears", I had them pinned back. Did it change me? Yes, it did. My confidence level was higher and I didn't feel unattractive. If a cosmetic procedure will enhance not only your looks, but your inner confidence—go for it.

Should you consider cosmetic surgery?

Self-esteem is one of the elements, which makes up the foundation of one's ego. (Here is the shrink speaking)—My opinion has always been "do as you wish—only if it will make YOU fell better". Be cautious not to get into the every 6-month "nip and tuck" syndrome—dangerous—see a shrink first.

Let's also hit on 'competition' for a moment.

There is no competition. Why? Because no one looks exactly like you—and you look like you—not them—get it?! So competition is a very subjective word. Casting is a very subjective profession— and as I mentioned in an earlier chapter—no one ever knows why they didn't book a job—assuming all candidates were equal in their acting skills. Remember the story of the actress whom the director felt had "one lazy eye?"—I rest my case.

In closing out this chapter, my sense is—if you are 'obsessed' with having some work done, then do it. Do it for yourself and don't bother with what anyone else thinks.

Be advised that any change physically will alter you internally.

Any ethical cosmetic surgeon will cross examine you as to reasons why you feel you need work done.

We are in the 21st century when now, more than ever, men are having just as much work done as women.

By the way, should you decide to have surgery performed—less is more and the best compliment you could be given "post" surgery is "how rested you look"—(face lift). Cosmetic surgery should enhance gently, not radically.

One more consideration in changing one's looks as one ages. Do you as an actor wish to grow older naturally and broaden your roles? If you have played 35 year old for many years and you are now 50, do you wish to go into different roles or try for those 35 year old one? In my opinion, there are enough actors legitimately 35 years old.

Academy Award winner, Shelley Winters, one of the beauties of her time and a great actress, just "let herself be herself ". it didn't hurt her career—same goes for Gregory Peck, Paul Newman and so many others.

Again—think before you "cut"!! and good luck!

CHAPTER TWENTY-FIVE

Getting Personal With Jerry*

Some personal answers from Jerry *these questions were asked of me by Eric Vollweiler, a college student at Emerson College in Boston, Massachusetts—and about 100 other people throughout my career!

Favorite all time actors: Spencer Tracey/Tom Hanks Favorite all time actress Meryl Streep, Bette Davis Classiest actor Cary Grant, Raphael Spbarge Classiest actress—Audrey Hepburn, Leslie Hope Favorite films: Forrest Gump, The Shawshank Redemption, The Godfather 1, Casablanca, Citizen Kane q) Had you become an actor, whom would you have emulated? a) Tim Robbins with Alec Baldwin's head on Tim's body.

Favorite Network Executive: Brandon Tartikoff (1949-1997),

Former President NBC Entertainment Most influence on your career— Mike Donohew, Al Onorato, Ron Meyer, Renee Valente, Ruta Lee, Debbie Reynolds

Best ensemble casting: The Today Show *my editor argued this answer with me. Why do I consider The Today Show the best ensemble casting? My answer is that typically the best ensembles of which there have been and are many hold an audience's interest for a 1/2 hour or one hour. The Today Show holds audience's attention for 15 hours per week.

Questions and Answers from 25 years of teaching and public speaking: Q) Why did you become a casting director? Because secretly, I always wanted to be a song and dance man. BUT—I didn't have the talent. I have always looked up to and admired actors because of their skills and risk-taking. I have always loved working with actors to this date. Also, because of my love of the 85 "So You Wanna Be An Actor . . . Act Like One" human emotions—and the respect for people who can open their mouths and make a writer's line and character come to life—an extraordinary gift. Q) What do you like most about your job and what don't you like about your job? I love meeting new talent and watching them grows. What I don't like is the "judgment calls" that must go along with my profession. Q) Out of all of your projects thus far, are there any moments, events that are "Hallmark" moments? The opportunity to work with Lucille Ball, Bob Hope, Robert Mitchum, Lana Turner, Fred MacMurray, Robert Preston, Ann-Margret, Lisa Minelli, and thousands of other actors, Marvin Hamlisch, Presidents Ford and Reagan, Julian Bond, and the Hallmark of all—Colin Powell have made me realize how lucky I am in my chosen profession.

Q) What is the singles best piece of advice that you can give to an actor? Always be honest, keep your integrity and think before you speak.

Q) If an actor has not had a chance to look over the sides for whatever reason, should he ask for extra time, and if so, how much?
With all of the state of the art ways to obtain sides (on line, facsimile, in person) there is little excuse for not receiving sides.
However, there are exceptions. In this particular case, I think two hours is enough time for an actor to study and make choices on material.

Q) Do you frown on an actor who tries to change his appointment time for a personal reason? Absolutely not. If an actor has a legitimate reason for wishing to change an appointment time "fine—just don't abuse the privilege.

Q) What's the best thing to do after giving your reading? Is there anything or should I just say thank you & leave? Thank the people in the office and leave if they want you to read material again they will ask. NEVER EVER ask to read for another role. (See chapter ay Goodnight Gracie) Q) What's the best way to get a GOOD agent? In this day and age, the best shot at getting a good agent is to have tape or a DVD or VCR on yourself. One might luck out and have an agent see them in a play or workshop or college production. Q) How does an actor find his/her most marketable qualities and then utilize them to their fullest? I think that we all know what our most marketable qualities are. My teeth, smile and sense of humor have done wonders for me. I look at the eyes first—choose your best quality and soar with it. Perhaps you have an engaging personality, perhaps you have special eyes, voice, style of dress—only you know what shines best about yourself.

Q) When preparing for an interview, how should I dress? Dress in the manner in which you would go to any professional meeting. That does not mean high heels or suit and tie, breasts exposed or inappropriate attire, like a bathing suit, shorts, etc.

Q) Say you're doing a speech in an office for someone and it's not necessarily directed toward an audience, is an advantage/ disadvantage to cheat your eye toward the auditor? I believe you are talking about a onologue I personally do not like to be the focal point of a monologue I prefer studying the actor. The best practice I have found is to ask. If the person to whom you are reading does not wish to be the focal point, then find one—a pencil on the desk—a piece of furniture, or perhaps a hanging on the wall.

Q) On perhaps the second or third callback when you're really familiar with the material (sides) should you just hold it or once or twice look down at it or look at it only if you forget your place. Never ever read without holding a side in your hand.

Actors are not required to memorize material before they get on the set. It doesn't matter whether or not you know the material with your eyes closed always hold your sides (material).

Q) If you've read a piece one way for the auditioners and they are willing to have you do it again in another manner, how far is it prudent to go with it? A few twists or something out on another limb? Use your brains and listen. When the auditioner suggests another way to read the scene, LISTEN and be clear.

Ask if you do not understand what they are looking for. Always remember that less is more. Don't overact, don't get stagy, and use your own instinct. Q) When reading with a casting director, is it ever advisable to suggest a change in the way he or she is reading to you if you see in that will help your reading? Casting directors are not actors. One of the most frequent complaints actors have is that the reader is looking down at the material and not at the actor. NEVER suggest to anyone reading with you how they should read do the best you can and do not let the reader's lack of acting ability deter you from doing good work.

Q) Why do casting directors have all these horror stories of actors who commit cardinal sins at auditions? Obviously, these actors are being called in. WHY are they being called in? I've never committed a single faux pas in the entire 37 years I've been acting, and I get called in roughly as often as elections are held. What gives? This is one of the downfalls of acting. In the 21st century aside from the reality shows, most demographics ask for and younger faces, this is not to say that there is not enough work for a more mature actor there is it is just that the competition gets heavier as one ages.

Q) Is there an unspoken actors caste system? With rare exception, actors who are on top seem to have always been on top, no matter how mediocre they or their films might get. 99% of actors who take smaller roles in films seem never to be heard from again. Who's behind this? Martians? The brotherhood of masons with their secret handshakes? What's going on here? If there is an unspoken caste system, someone might tell me about it. I think not. The actors on top all started on the bottom do your research Matt Damon and Ben Affleck didn't just appear and win an Oscar. They had study and work behind them.

Q) What qualities do you look for in actor's performance, personality and character? One thing—believability.

Q) If you were an actor in Hollywood, how would you pursue your career? What means would you use? If I were an actor in Hollywood, I would study hard enough until I was ready to go on auditions and then do theatre and hope to be seen by an agent, casting director or producer. Someone will see someone in a theatre production and the career will take off.

Q) Can you detect a future as well as exceptional actors (or rather who will be the exceptional ones)? I'm no psychic, but any casting director who has instinct will immediately recognize an actor's ability.

Q) What is the best way for a starting actor to conduct himself on the set? Keep quiet and keep still, listen and watch and stay out of the way until you are called for your scene. It's called learning.

Q) What is the single most important thing an actor should know and be prepared for in an audition? An actor should only come in with honesty with himself and as the character.

Q) Do you like "ICS" (Interesting choices that aren't necessarily) indicated in the script? This is a new one on me. I've never heard the expression. Ask the casting director or director if you might stretch the character—if they say, fine go with it otherwise, use your head and make the appropriate choices.

Q) Do you have any particular technique that you know works for actors to calm oneself—or focus before an audition? Actors have different ways of calming themselves down. I don't think there is one stock answer. For me, when I need to deliver a speech and sense some stage fright I typically turn the fear into concentration and focus on what I am going to be discussing in front of the audience.

Q) Would you prefer people to get physical or to demonstrate behavior or rather to sit and simply connect? Less is more: just be the character or just be yourself. If material indicates physicality, NEVER ever touch a reader (casting director, director, etc). Just be in the moment and don't become overly dramatic.

Q) What tips can you offer to an aspiring actor when one has an 8-hour day-job?

Good question. I would be upfront with your boss and advise that there may be days that you will have to leave for appointments.

Perhaps you could rade your lunch hour at noon for a reading or meeting at 3pm. Don't lie—tell the truth most bosses who hire actors are used to the appointments during the day.

Q) When dealing with agents, what qualities do you prefer they have, whom do you like to deal with? All I ask for is honesty. I have relied on agents through my entire career to guide me to the right actors. If an agent burns me by sending an actor I've not met into my office and the actor should not be out on auditions, I let the agent get by once—hurt me once, shame on you—hurt me twice, shame on me.

Q) How often should we keep in touch with postcards? I personally like the postcard system. It is recommended strongly that actors NOT phone a casting office. Drop in's are also frowned upon. A postcard when you are appearing on TV or in a stage production or have changed representation or contact information is the perfect opportunity for a mailing. Q) Would you consider hiring an actor that doesn't have representation (an agent?) Granted that you saw their work and liked it? I've always had an open door policy. If I see a photo I like or a resume I find interesting; it doesn't matter to me. Better yet; if I see an actor in a stage production or in another vehicle, of course it doesn't matter whether or not he/she has any representation.

Q) Do you and other casting directors hold grudges against actors because of their relationships with an agent you don't like?

I can only speak for myself. I hold no grudges ever. I've had one or two occasions over the years that I've asked an actor to leave my office and these were the most isolated incidences when they rashed" auditions!—A Big fat no no!

Q) Do you frown upon extra work? And if so, why? Not only do I not frown upon extra work, I think its' a good learning tool.

Up and coming actors have to make a living the money is good, but more than that, you get to see how projects come to fruition and get to watch other actors work more learning. I totally support extra work

Q) If you are not SAG how is the best way to get a theatrical agent? It doesn't matter whether you are SAG or not. The 21st century is the toughest time I remember in getting representation. Having tape is a solid bet, and even that sometimes doesn't get one an agent.

Q) If you do not have a theatrical agent, how is the (I'm sure he means to say, "what is" but nevertheless) best way to get auditions with casting directors? I commented in the chapter on gents that this is the most frequently asked question. There is no way to out guess who will or will not be in an audience. I still say, do theatre and daytime drama then send out mass mailings or postcards and do mass mailings of headshots and resumes, two or three times a year statistically, someone will call you in for an appointment. no? Say you? That doesn't work? Pray hard!

Q) Do you think the "2-for photo (2 smaller headshots on the 8x10) is a good preferable to 2-8x10 different headshots? I'm amazed at the expression. The 8 x 10, plain old black and white is fine—see the chapter on photos Q) Do you like to cast "against type" when the actor does a great job to convince you to? Duh—yes. I've always supported from the earliest days nontraditional casting. There is no reason that a woman cannot be anything a man can be except a father and vice versa

Q) Do you prefer casting actors with more TV and Film credits than without? Of course, we all want to hire actors with experience, BUT, this does not mean that I who support the theatre actor will not cast theatre actors

Q) Do you like to use actors that you like more than once? I've re-hired actors over the years if they are right for a role, they get called in, whether I've worked with them once or 10 times

Q) As a casting director please give advice on how an actor can upgrade their status. Meaning if an actor were considered in the under-five category and/or afternoon drama category only, how would we impress and or convince those powers that be that we can do mainstream? A casting director can look at tape of something an under actor has done. Every actor I know started out with a one liner including Harrison Ford and David Hasselhoff

Q) Do producers (to the best of your knowledge) make judgments on actors brought in on their resume Representation?

Meaning, does a producer assume an actor is better, not just by the actors audition, but by who is his representation and who hired him before? I think it is obvious that if an actor is represented by a high-powered large agency, the agent sees something in them. However, that does not play in my office.

Many casting directors bring in actors from the smallest agencies in the city. Have a good photo and honest resume; the name or status of the agent will not interfere in most casting offices.

Q) There is an "A" list of actors, which means there must be a "B" list. Is there a "C" "D" and "E" list? How do you start? How do you move up? In all honesty, patience, time and luck, providing you can act. Q) What would you think makes a good actor other than the obvious? (A special trait) Tough question.

See the chapter on A Gift From God

Q) How open-minded are you about seeing actors as entirely different characters? (Do you have a tendency to type cast)?
(Honestly) See above answer re non-traditional casting). And that's honest!

Q) Is there any way that is not bothersome to the average casting director to get feedback after an audition? No—it is awkward for a c.d. to give feedback. A cordial thank you is nice—if a c.d. is overwhelmed by your performance, you will be acknowledged verbally or by a callback

Q) Since I have been in the biz for only 3 years, and my age range is early to mid-thirties, people assume my resume represents 10 or 12 years in the business—so it seems relatively weak. When they take the time to find out my resume represents only 3 years, then they've impressed. How should I handle this? I sense that you are telling me that people are impressed with your ability even though you have only been acting for three years. Take the compliments and don't worry about what is on your resume

Q) Are there any extra tips or things I can do to get more auditions for feature films and MOW's? It's all in a look—that's as honest as I can be. Film actors have film faces TV actors have TV faces what's the difference you ask? The difference is that a film face jumps off the screen or one cannot take their eyes off of some one.

Q) If you are with a good agent and have a chance to move up to a bigger agent, when do you know its' best to move up? This is one of the best questions of the day. I am a strong believer in loyalty. I think I will give you the answer that Cuba Gooding, Jr. said when receiving his Oscar. He thanked his first agent, Lorilee, Jr., for her support and also for guiding him to the right agent when his career started taking off. Agents are typically interested in money and how much you can make for them. If you like your agent and trust your agent, stay with your agent.

When an actor is hot, casting directors will find you whether you are with William Morris Agency or Minnie Mouse Agency.

Q) How important is videotape? In this day and age, it is vital.

Be advised that DVD's are now taking the place of inch just as inch took the place of inch videotape. Typically, agents will ask for tape before working with an actor and videotape is an invaluable tool for casting directors in making decisions. Q)

Does it do any good to mail a picture and resume to a casting director for a show you think you are right for? I can only speak for myself. Unsolicited mailings have always been welcomed in my offices you have nothing to lose. I personally open every single envelope other casting directors may just work with agents but the only thing you can lose is a photo and resume in a wastebasket.

Q) How can I get more readings for feature films? Submit a photo and resume that honestly represents you patience, time and luck again prevail.

Q) What can I do to get my agent more excited about me? Keep booking jobs

Q) Do you handle submissions directly and how do you process them? All envelopes with submissions whether by agents, personal managers or unsolicited are opened and reviewed. They are stacked into categories, usually who looks right for a role and those stacks of photos are reviewed and culled down sometimes more than a dozen times before I select my typically 5 choices per role.

Q) Do personalities keep you from hiring someone? I believe I answered this question earlier; I have had two isolated incidences of personality clashes

Q) What key points should an actor remember before entering an audition?

See cheat sheet and just be yourself in the character's body.

CHAPTER TWENTY-SIX

No Limitations Please

— — — — —

Actors have far too many "excuses" in my opinion. If it's not one thing, it's another—so I wanted to discuss "limitations" with you. Soar With Your Strengths, a book by my pal Paula Nelson is a great title which applies to all of us. If you are going to try to succeed as an actor OR in any other profession, please don't go in with "limitations" placed on yourself.

I went to a fundraising event last week which reminded me to add these few pages on a very sensitive topic. That being— medical or emotional "issues" or problems which might stand in an actor's way.

I use the word issues because some people deal with disorders in one way or another. I have worked with actors are visually or hearing impaired, HIV positive, full blown AIDS—and those dealing with cancer or diabetes.

The event last week was to raise funds for Turrets syndrome—a very distressing disorder caused by lack of "synapses" in the brain. It makes one inappropriately scream obsenities or "gibberish"—and/or leaves the person with jerking movements of the arms—blinking eyes and all sorts of physical "quirks".

Turrets syndrome falls into the category of OCD conditions— Obsessive, compulsive disorders.

Other areas which actor's must deal are—Down syndrome, dyslexia, ADD (Adult deficit disorder) stuttering, lisp, panic attacks, stage fright, fear of flying—any "limitation" which might alter their career or life style to a degree which is totally non-productive.

I have worked with actors suffering from and/or dealing with all of the above. Thankfully, now in the 21st century, the pharmaceutical world of wonders helps countless millions of people all over the world with all of the aforementioned problems.

When I was 12 years old, I went on a school trip to New York City, a two hour trip from the Jersey shore—where Danny DeVito, Jack Nicholson, Bruce Springsteen and I spent our 'growing up' years.

Upon my return to the school ground where my Dad waited for my twin sister and me to depart from our respective buses, I stepped into a world of 42 years of hell. Panic attack, ODC, agoraphobia. Life altering "issues" due to what we now know is chemical deficiencies in the brain and are easily treatable.

Kim Basinger with whom I worked on "From here To Eternity" TV series—and the very talented, bright and gifted Donny Osmond, my pal Florence Henderson (Mrs. Brady) a couple of very successful politicians I am acquainted with—and the list goes on. All of us have gone through the same kind of hell. Was it limiting to us? Yes—very—and here we all are to talk about it.

The point is—get help with whatever "issues" you have. There is help out there for everyone—new meds for migraines, PMS, alcoholism, drug addiction and the big mama of all "depression".

I often wonder if some of the actors from the 1920's to the 1980's suffering from alcoholism and drug addiction, complexes we have never heard of—all due to chemical imbalances would have been better actors? I sense so.

In the old days, those of us suffering from chemical imbalances were thrown into the category of schizophrenia—today, everything is lumped into bi-polar disorders. Why even bother to discuss this topic? Because for those of you hiding in the 97 "So You Wanna Be An Actor . . . Act Like One" closet or suffering from whatever—bulimia and other eating disorders, depression, post partum or generalized—get help—it is readily available.

Don't ever be afraid to let the casting director or assistant director on the set know that you have "special needs" like— insulin intake, drops for your eyes if you happen to have glaucoma—you get my message.

Stop hiding behind your dyslexia—get your sides early and see you Doctor. Tom Cruise is a big time dyslexic actor and has dealt with it.

Michael J. Fox suffers from Parkinson's disease and continues to make appearance—despite his "limitation".

If you are not well and have an interview—tell your agent— change the appointment. A sensitive casting director will clearly understand. If you are working and ill—tough titty—the show must go on. Too many famous stories to relate about the Gene Kelly's of the world whose dance in the rain with 102-degree temperature—didn't stop production—and the film is today considered the number one musical of all time. (See Imdb. com—Singing' In The Rain).

You are NOT going to kill your chances of booking a role if you have to take a break for an insulin shot.

Having sat on the California governor's Committee on Disabilities, it was with the late Ethel Winant, Paul Waginer and others that we pushed through legislation and awareness in the industry—why couldn't a wheelchair bound actor sit behind a desk and play any given number of roles? Why couldn't a hearing impaired actor work?

My buddy Carrie Fisher "came out of the closet" with her chemical imbalances—and now under control—she leads a very happy and productive life.

Is there help for any actor with any type of "limitation"?

Obviously, just don't stand in your own way.

No excuses.

When my own chemical imbalances were replaced by a magic bullet medication my physician discovered in 1999, my entire life changed. When sharing the news of this remarkable find with a confidante, I said "I have no idea how I got through school" and she replied "school"—how the hell did you get through life?"

NO LIMITATIONS PERMITTED—you are in a profession with no boundaries—just don't ever limit yourselves!! jf

READ YOUR SIDES IN THE WAITING ROOM AND STOP "COMPARING" IF EVERYONE WERE NOT DIFFERENT IN SOME WAY-CASTING WOULD BE A LOTTERY

MRS. REAGAN/MRS. FORD/ THE WORD CANCER AND IN PARTICULAR BREAST CANCER WAS NOT DISCUSSED IN THE 80'S-NOT UNLIKE AIDS IN THE BEGINNING-SOME OF YOU READING THIS BOOK HAVE NO IDEA OF HOW PRIMITIVE WE ARE ABOUT CERTAIN SUBJECTS-AUTISM HAS JUST COME OUT OF THE CLOSET-AND BELIEVE IT OR NOT-I PUT TWO OF MY STUDENTS IN A PRODUCTION OF 'GREASE' AND THEY DID JUST FINE!!

THERE ARE PAST AND PRESENT ACTORS WHO "HIDE" ILLNESS FOR FEAR THAT THEY WON'T WORK ONCE THE WORD GETS OUT-ODDLY ENOUGH-TIMES HAVE CHANGED-MICHAEL J. FOX HAS A NEW SERIES ON THE AIR-WE HIRED A WONDERFUL ACTRESS NAMED MADELYN RHUE FOR MANY EPISODES OF 'FAME' AND WORKED AROUND HER DISABILITY-SHE WAS SUFFERING FROM M.S.-WE HIRED A BLIND ACTRESS IN A COURTROOM SCENE-AND NO ONE EVER KNEW THAT SHE HAD NO SIGHT-

THE MEDIA ACCESS OFFICE COMES TO BEING!

Printed in the United States
By Bookmasters